WITCHY RESERVATIONS

MYSTIC INN MYSTERIES

STEPHANIE DAMORE

PINK SAPPHIRE PRESS

To Dad,
For your love and encouragement

CHAPTER ONE

"Nailed it," Lacey said when we were the last two people remaining in the boardroom. "I don't know how you do it. No one closes more deals than you. I swear, it's magic," my friend and associate quipped.

"Magic?" I scoffed. "Hard work and determination are more like it."

"Whatever you say. But Dower Corp. was ready to book their convention at the Westin until you convinced them to talk to us first. Next thing you know, boom! Half a million-dollar contract for us. First the corner office and the next it'll be the top floor. You'll be an executive yet."

I beamed under my associate's praise. "Well, let's not jinx it. They haven't signed yet."

"But you know they will," Lacey said.

I didn't want to admit it, but I'd be shocked at this

point if they didn't. I didn't have time to dwell on that success, though. I had a lunch meeting with another potential client in twenty minutes, and I'd be lucky not to be late with Chicago's traffic.

"Where's the United file?" I asked Lacy after reaching my desk. I lifted up my leather padfolio and searched for the folder below it, but came up empty. With any luck, the airline would be hosting its elite members for a luxury weekend at the hotel before whisking their A-list fliers off to exotic locations. That is if I ever made it to the meeting on time.

"Oh, sorry about that. I think it's on my desk. Let me go grab it." Lacey walked briskly out of my office.

There was a knock on my door as Kevin, my assistant, peeked his head in.

"How'd it go?" he asked.

"Great, I think. They didn't sign yet, but I'm pretty sure we got them." I smiled as I continued scrambling for my next meeting. "They said they'd call with their decision shortly. Do not let that phone go to voicemail." I pointed to the multiline telephone that sat on my desk. A couple of red lights blinked back, alerting me to a voicemail and another caller on the line.

"About that. There's someone on the line that needs to speak with an Angelica?"

I stopped dead at the use of my formal name. The blood rushed out of my head. I steadied my fingertips on my desk.

"They said it was an emergency. Something about your aunt?"

"Okay, thanks. I'll take it from here."

Kevin nodded and ducked back out of my office. I scrambled after him to shut the door and raced back for the phone before anyone else accidentally picked up the call.

"Hello?" I spoke fast, and my voice sounded raspy.

"Angelica, is that you? Heaven's child. I can barely hear you. Hello?" the older woman's voice said.

"It's me, Clemmie," I said, recognizing my aunt's best friend on the other line. I hadn't spoken to her in a decade but had known her most of my life. "What's wrong?"

"Well, I'm afraid your aunt's time has come. She's asked me to call you home to say goodbye."

I closed my eyes and shook my head. "What are you talking about? Aunt Thelma is fine." She had to be. Nothing bad could ever happen to her. She was one powerful witch, and I was convinced she would live forever.

"I'm sorry, honey. You need to come home."

"What? You're not making any sense." I lowered my voice even more. "What about Constance? She's still around, isn't she?"

"There are some things that even magic can't heal. Can I tell her you're on your way?"

I nodded before finding my voice. "Yeah. I'll leave right now."

"Oh, and Angelica?"

"Yeah?"

"Hocus pocus."

"What?"

"New password to get into town."

Oh, yeah. "Got it." I didn't bother to write the words down.

THE GOOD THING about living near one of the world's busiest airports is that you can almost guarantee a same-day flight to any place in the continental United States. Instead of meeting with United, I took one of its direct flights from Chicago to Atlanta.

Feet back on southern soil and rental car keys in hand, I got behind the wheel of a white Mercedes-Benz and headed southeast toward Silverlake. It had been thirteen years since I'd been back, and my aunt's dying wish was the only thing that could ever make me return.

Not that she was really dying.

I loved my aunt. Growing up, she was all that I had, and I wouldn't believe she was on her deathbed until I saw her with my own two eyes. Us Nightingale women were a stubborn bunch.

I guess I would soon see for myself. In a little over an hour, I'd be back in my hometown. My stomach

filled with dread as I repeated the words in my head
—hometown.

Silverlake was enchanted. No, really. You wouldn't
find the town on a map or listed on any tourist website.
That is, unless you were a witch. Witches were sure to
have heard of it, but the good old normal folk—mortals
—wouldn't see it even if it was right in front of them
thanks to the charms placed on the land. Not to
mention the secret password, and even that changed
with the seasons. No, Silverlake was a supernatural safe
haven, a place where visitors and residents could
escape the restrictive real world and be free to be who
they truly were—witches.

As I navigated my highway exchange, curving off of
I-75 and venturing onto the back road that would lead
me straight to the enchanted town, my cell phone rang,
and I saw that it was Allen, my boyfriend of sorts. We
weren't putting a label on it, and that was perfectly fine
by me. Our relationship was very new, and what were
we anyway, teenagers? Did people even refer to each
other as boyfriend and girlfriend anymore? Well,
regardless of the title, I had to take the call.

"Hello?" I said while being careful to keep my eyes
on the road.

"Angela? Is everything all right? Your assistant told
me you had to go out of town for a family emergency."

I cursed Kevin under my breath, wishing he
wouldn't have even said as much. I worked hard to keep

my past separate from my present, and I wasn't about to let those wires cross anytime soon, if ever.

"Yeah, I did. It's okay, I'm only going to be gone for the weekend. Do you want to meet for dinner Sunday night?" Allen was silent on the other end of the line. "Allen? Are you still there?"

"It's just that Paulina's isn't open on Sunday evenings."

"Oh, that's right." Paulina's was Allen's favorite restaurant. Make that the only restaurant we ever went to. What could I say? The man had high standards and a taste for fine Italian dining that only Paulina's could deliver. "Maybe next Friday then."

"Next Friday it is. You have an enjoyable visit with your family, and I look forward to reconnecting when you return."

"So do I. Have a good weekend." I hung up and tossed my phone onto the passenger seat, where it landed with a soft plop before I reached for it once more. "Siri," I said to my phone's personal assistant, "remind me to send Kevin an email in an hour."

"I'll add it to your calendar," the automated voice responded.

"Thank you." It was time to remind my assistant to keep his mouth shut, especially to guys I was dating.

CHAPTER TWO

I n no time at all, my car idled in front of the dilapidated one-lane covered bridge that led to Silverlake. The rickety structure looked like it could barely support a pedestrian's weight, let alone a car, and that was by design. Any sane person who faced that bridge would turn around and find an alternative route. I looked through the old bridge at the barren field that lay ahead. To the average eye, it looked like an abandoned cotton field. You could make out where the rows of crops had once been, but now all that was left was hard-packed mounds of dirt and dried-up sticks. In the distance stood a weathered gray barn. The frame of one anyway. A substantial chunk of the roof was missing, as were more than a few sideboards, the farmer and his family long since moving on to greener pastures. Or more fruitful ones anyway.

I powered down the window. A wall of thick,

humid air greeted me. My neck instantly felt sticky, and my dark hair started to frizz. I gathered my hair with one hand and pulled it over behind my shoulder.

"Hello?" I hollered out the window. "It's Angelica Nightingale." My formal name sounded foreign coming from my lips. "Is anyone out there?"

A soft popping noise preceded the sudden appearance of Mr. McCormick, who must now be a town guardian by the way he appeared out of thin air. That wasn't a spell any old witch was allowed to cast, even if they were skilled enough, which I wasn't. Legislation kept a tight rein on who could disappear and reappear in a snap. The greenhouse manager dusted the dirt off his overalls. "Sorry about that, I was just watering the petunias. My word, is that you, Angelica? How many moons has it been since you've been back? I'll have to tell Molly you're in town," the manager said, referencing his daughter, who was my age. We had attended every grade from kindergarten through high school together, along with the other seventeen kids in my class, but that didn't mean I wanted a reunion.

"Oh, no. I'm just popping in for a quick visit. Um, hocus locus?"

Mr. McCormick waved the password away. "You don't need a password. You're a local. The bridge will remember you. Just drive right through."

"Thanks."

"Oh, and Angelica? Give our best to your aunt. We've been thinking of her."

I nodded, unable to find the right words to respond. "She's fine," I repeated under my breath but couldn't ignore the lump that formed in my throat. I gently pushed down on the gas and hoped Mr. McCormick was right and the bridge would remember. I felt the wood creak uncomfortably under the weight of the front tires, and I couldn't help ducking as the car pulled inside the bridge. Ahead of me, all I could see was dirt and scrub, but as soon as the back tires crossed from pavement onto wood, the scene before me changed. Everything was fresh, green, and vibrant despite it being the height of summer in Georgia. A smooth road picked up where the bridge ended. Thick, green grass and rolling hills filled the landscape along with mature pecan trees, full of fruit, and Peach Creek, which was really more like a river, ran along the driver's side window. As I came around the third bend, the town came into view. A curved iron sign suspended above the road welcomed visitors to Silverlake. The sign twinkled like pixie dust in the sunlight. The river continued to wind on the far left side of the property, cutting under the old wooden bridge and weaving off into the distance. It looked like the river kept going on forever. Only I knew better.

Straight ahead was the shopping district, Village Square. Wishing Well Park, with its lush yard, stood before the storybook shops. A white cast-iron fountain, with two tiers topped by a figure of a robed woman holding a staff, stood in the middle, acting as a focal point. Its majestic beauty enticed visitors to stop by and make a wish. Every month the coins were gathered up and donated to charity. A sidewalk outlined the park's perimeter, and wooden benches invited patrons to sit for a minute. The rest of the lawn left plenty of room for an afternoon picnic or nap under one of the impressive pecan trees.

Traffic moved around the park in a clockwise motion. I turned left and continued around the green space. When the road ended before the shops, I turned left once more and drove over a small bridge that again crossed Peach Creek.

I couldn't count how many times I'd played in the creek as a kid. Or even as a cat, splashing my paws in the cool water. A spell I didn't even know if I could pull off anymore. Instinctively, my hand reached up for my old tiger's eye pendant. Of course it wasn't there. It had been far too long since I'd done any transformation work. At one time, I had been rather good at it, but that was another lifetime ago. One I tried the last thirteen years to forget.

A matching footbridge was to the right outside my window. I'd run across that bridge as a child to sneak a piece of homemade fudge or a praline before supper. Just don't let Martha, the inn's cook, catch you. Nothing made her madder than a child spoiling her dinner. Behind me now was the outdoor shopping center. The mall was a little neighborhood in its own way. Connected storefronts were painted various colors—

buttery yellow, creamy ivory, robin's egg blue. They all looked different, but the colors were painted with the same intensity, which helped tie it all together, as did the winding flagstone path that meandered down the streets that created the small village. The shopping district was foot traffic only. If guests were lucky, they could snag a parking spot up front along the storefronts. If not, they would have to park in one of the lots to the right of Village Square and walk over to the shops, making the front parking spots coveted by visitors and locals alike.

The road curved to the right across the bridge and continued around Silverlake, which the spring-fed creek washed into. And it was around the first bend where my aunt's hotel sat—The Mystic Inn.

It was hard to describe the overwhelming feeling that hit me as soon as the inn came into view. The three-story building was Bavarian in style. The timber-framed exterior was painted soft white with dark brown trim and accent work. The doorframe was curved, like the windows. Walnut-stained planter boxes overflowed with ivy and blooms in various shades of purple underneath the second story windows. A grassy knoll separated the front of the inn from the main road, dampening any roadside noise, not that there ever was any traffic. I pulled into the parking lot, and my heart began beating erratically in my chest as if it was skipping a beat. Aunt Thelma had to be okay. I hadn't mentally prepared myself for what I was about to face, and truth be told, I might not have had the courage to show up if I had. Oh yeah, I was definitely one who would rather run away from my feelings than face them. It was a character trait that I wasn't proud of, but I was well aware of. I looked up at the building and swallowed. I hadn't even asked Clemmie where Aunt Thelma was. It was as if I drove to the inn on autopilot, and now I wasn't sure where to go. Should I go inside or continue around the lake to the small community hospital?

I decided to stop inside first.

I pulled into a guest parking spot. I was sure someone inside would tell me where I needed to be if I could only muster up the courage to ask. I took a deep breath, unbuckled my seatbelt, and shrieked when Aunt Thelma yanked open the car door and greeted me with a bear hug.

"Aunt Thelma?" I broke free from my aunt's embrace and took a solid look at the person before me. "I thought you were dying?" The woman before me looked anything but. In fact, she looked twenty years younger than I remembered her.

"Oh, this?" Thelma used her index finger to circle her face. "This is just an age-defying potion, nothing really. Wait until you see Clemmie."

"I'm not talking about your face. We can discuss that later. I'm talking about Clemmie's phone call telling me to get home as soon as possible."

"Oh, balderdash. How else was I supposed to get you here? You keep ghosting me."

"Ghosting you?"

"See, I'm hip with the lingo. Isn't that what you kids call it these days? Not returning calls?"

I stepped out of the car and adjusted my blouse. "Aunt Thelma, I was really worried about you."

"Good. That means you still care. Now come, give me a hand."

My feet obeyed even though my emotions had yet to catch up. "I knew you were okay. Wait until I see Clemmie," I said more to myself than anyone else as we walked to the door.

"What's that, dear?"

"Nothing." But then I did remember something. "Why has Mr. McCormick been thinking of you? He told me to give you his best."

Aunt Thelma waved the concern away. "I told him I had food poisoning. I wanted to keep up the ruse all the way to the end. Just in case."

"You're unbelievable."

"What? It worked." Aunt Thelma had no shame.

We walked into the hotel, and I stopped short in the lobby. The place looked exactly how I remembered it—and that wasn't a good thing. White-tiled flooring and cracked gray Formica countertops were the first things I noticed, followed by the thick silver and satiny wallpaper peeling behind the front desk to my right. Handfuls of local brochures advertising canoe rentals, shopping discounts, and dining coupons were thrown haphazardly on a side table. An oscillating desk fan did little to help as it threatened to blow them all on the floor. As it was, a couple had already landed there, and no one had bothered to pick them up.

Not to mention it wasn't much cooler inside the lobby than it had been outside. I blew upwards on my forehead to help cool myself off, and it didn't even remotely help. I was about to ask about the air-conditioning when a loud rumble that sounded like screws cascading down a metal sheet interrupted me.

"Ice maker?" I asked, furrowing my brow. The machine had been on its last leg for years. How it managed to spit out anything that even resembled cubed ice at this point was beyond me. Aunt Thelma raised her eyebrows and nodded her head.

Straight ahead was a set of glass doors that led out to the patio, with the beach and lake beyond that. At least the view was timeless. I couldn't say the same thing about the lobby decor. The seating area was arranged like a living room with a big, boxy projector-type television as the focal point. The sixty-inch TV was the type that had been popular and expensive in the nineties but now just looked dated.

"Now, do you see why I need your help?" my aunt asked.

"You could've just asked."

"I would've if you would've returned my calls."

I bit my lip. Aunt Thelma had been right. I had

been ghosting her, to use her term. "I'm sorry. Work has been stupid busy lately, and I'm seeing this new guy—"

"A man? You have a man in your life?" Aunt Thelma's eyes twinkled mischievously.

"It's really new. I shouldn't have said anything."

"Is he a shifter?"

"No!" I shot back as if the suggestion was absurd.

"Witch? I know you have a thing for witches. You remember Vance?"

I was not about to talk about my high school ex-boyfriend. Thank the stars he didn't live in Silverlake anymore. I brought the conversation to the present. "No. Allen's completely normal."

"Normal? What fun is that?" Aunt Thelma held her hand up in a questioning gesture.

"He's an accountant. Does the books for the hotel I work at."

Aunt Thelma wrinkled her nose. "You're worse off than I thought."

"I am not!" I said with more force than I meant.

"Sure you're not."

Okay, so maybe I was working fifty hours with little recognition, and Allen was fond of routine. There's nothing wrong with eating at the same restaurant every Friday night and ordering the same meal. If you knew what you liked, why change?

"Hello? Earth to Angelica." Aunt Thelma waved her hand in front of my face.

"What?" I blinked a couple of times.

"How about we head to the office?"

"Sure." Maybe someplace private would be a good place to talk. I was suddenly aware of the curious eyes glancing our way as guests passed through the lobby.

I trailed after Aunt Thelma, behind the front counter, to where the back office was located. But when she opened the door for me to walk in, I couldn't believe my eyes.

I stared in shock at the mess. Mail was piled on the desk and spilled over onto the floor. An old, boxy computer took up the other half. It was the type of machine, yellowed with age, that probably ran Linux software and typed orange block letters on a black screen. I could picture the screen asking me to STRIKE Y TO PRINT OUT OR ENTER FACTORS. Shoved in the corner was a rotary phone. Over-sized, five-inch binders, dead spider plants, and dust bunnies competed for space on the back countertops.

"When's the last time you even opened this door?" I asked. It looked like someone had given up and just started shoving mail underneath the door.

"What year did you leave again?" Aunt Thelma asked.

"You've got to be kidding me."

"I told you before you left that the business side wasn't my strong suit."

"And I told you that you could easily learn or, better yet, hire someone."

"I guess I thought you'd be back. So I just shut the door." Aunt Thelma looked away so I wouldn't see her wipe away a stray tear. "I keep banishing the bills, but they just keep coming right back," she shook her head.

"Aunt Thelma, is the hotel in trouble?"

"Oh, no, no. Well ... maybe just a little bit." Aunt Thelma held her thumb and index finger an inch apart.

"How bad is it?"

"I honestly can't tell you. As you can see, I haven't run the numbers in years."

"Years?" Things were worse than I thought.

"I can't keep up with it anymore," Aunt Thelma confessed. "I don't even know where to begin."

My cell phone chirped in my hand. "I have to take this," I said, recognizing Lacey's number. I answered the call and stepped out of the office, walking straight out the door, back into the blazing sun.

"So, how's it going back home? Is your aunt okay?" Lacey asked.

I looked behind me at the inn. "She's fine."

"That's great!"

I stayed silent.

"That's not great?" Lacey sensed the hesitation on my end of the line.

I exhaled and felt a tension headache start to form. "No, it is. I just have a lot of work to do here."

"Well, I won't keep you. I just wanted to let you know that we got the convention! You always land them."

"That is excellent news."

"You'll be a VP before you know it."

"From your lips to God's ears. Listen, I have to let you go, but send the final contract for me to review, and then we can start issuing vendor agreements. Get the rooms blocked off and an estimated headcount for catering."

"Done and done. Check your email."

I heard the notification chime in my ear. "What would I do without you?"

"Just don't forget me when you're at the top."

"Never."

I hung up with Lacey and stared at the inn before me. Aunt Thelma was right—where to begin?

CHAPTER THREE

F our hours later, I came out of the back office, yawning and stretching. I had organized, cleaned, and rearranged the small space as much as I could. The computer was in desperate need of an upgrade. I ordered a new desktop model from a big box store one town over that offered curbside pickup, along with a desk chair because the one I'd been sitting on had seen better days. The wheels barely rolled, the height couldn't be adjusted, and the seat was torn, revealing dated yellow memory foam. Needless to say, my lower back was killing me.

"You're still back there working?" Aunt Thelma had turned the lobby television on to the Witch Network's nightly movie. A bowl of popcorn lay propped on her lap. Her feet stretched out between two chairs.

"I think I could keep at it for a week straight, and I

still wouldn't be done." The numbers were all running together, and I could sure use some backup.

"Why don't you call that accountant boyfriend of yours?"

"What? No. Um, ah," I stammered.

"I won't curse him, promise. Go on. We can keep the broom in the closet for a couple of days. Can't we?" Off in the distance, somewhere unseen, I heard the inn's resident ghost cackle.

"You might be able to, but what about Percy?" Percy the Poltergeist was ... difficult. "Not to mention that every business around here has a magical name, even if people didn't perform spells in front of him."

"Who says you need to take him into town? Hang out here at the hotel. Take the canoes out for a romantic trip around the lake. Dine alfresco under the stars. Think of how relaxing and romantic it could be," Aunt Thelma bounced her eyebrows.

I shook my head. "No way, not happening." I was keeping Allen as far away from Silverlake as possible.

"Well, that's too bad, seeing as I already invited him."

"You what?" That had to be a joke. "You did not." I almost tripped over my own two feet as part of me wanted to dash for my cell phone to call Allen, and the other wanted to race forward and wring my aunt's neck.

"Did so."

"How?"

"Magic," my aunt replied with a laugh.

"That's not funny."

"It's not meant to be. You're the one that said Allen was an accountant, so I gave him a call. It turns out he's more than agreeable to come for a visit. You're right. He is a lovely young man." My mouth opened and closed several times, but no words came out. "It's all arranged, and Percy has offered to pick him up from the airport Saturday morning."

"Percy? Percy the Poltergeist offered to help?" My voice was thick with doubt.

"Now, he hasn't thrown a fit in years."

"He's obnoxious!"

"Not so much anymore. Nowadays, it's more like Percy, the groundskeeper. Or Percy, my chauffeur. He drives me into the city at least once a month, if not more."

"Oh, that's very reassuring."

"He's a wonderful driver, and your friend won't see anything out of the ordinary. To him, Percy will look like a normal, nice old man picking him up at the airport."

"Percy?" Aunt Thelma hollered, setting her popcorn bowl down.

"Please, don't." I covered my eyes.

"Percy!" Aunt Thelma whistled as if she was calling a puppy.

I felt the tug on the end of my hair before Percy

materialized, blowing right through me and turning my veins into ice.

I shivered. "Must you do that?"

Percy may have died an old man, but he was a prankster at heart. "Can it be? Did Jelly come home to play? I thought you'd die before I saw you again."

"It's Angelica, and I'm not here to play," I said matter-of-factly.

"We'll see about that!" Percy blew a raspberry and floated through the lobby, knocking all the brochures off the counter in his wake.

"Oh yeah, he's real mature now," I replied to my aunt.

"Just give him a chance."

"I can't believe this is happening." I shook my head.

"Think of it as me doing you a favor."

"How is bringing Allen here and recruiting a poltergeist helpful?"

"What do you mean? Of course, it's helpful. How much time are you taking off work?" Aunt Thelma asked me.

"Thursday and Friday. I was planning on flying home Sunday." I didn't want to use up any more vacation time, but heaven knows I had weeks of it stored away.

"Right, and do you think you could get the books in order and everything fixed up around here in a handful of days?"

"No," I answered honestly.

"But with help, maybe you can."

I opened my mouth to protest some more but snapped it shut. I was arguing with the wrong person. The person I needed to reach was Allen. I turned away from the conversation, leaving my aunt to her movie, and retreated to the office to give Allen a call.

"Come on, pick up," I said to the phone as it rang. I danced my fingers on the side of my leg, waiting anxiously for our lines to connect, but the only thing that picked up was Allen's voicemail, which promptly told me that his mailbox was full. I resorted to shooting off a text, telling him that the trip was canceled and to call me as soon as possible. Hopefully, that would be enough to keep him in Chicago. I would try to reach him tomorrow morning in the office. Knowing Allen, he was sure to stop in there before taking off for the weekend. If anything, it would be to grab his favorite ten-key calculator.

I woke up the next morning still in the office, face down on the checkbook register. Sunlight filtered in through the blinds. I blinked for a few minutes trying to remember where I was. The last eighteen hours flooded back, and I closed my eyes and sighed. What a whirlwind of emotions yesterday had been. I'd need at least two cups of coffee before I'd be able to process it all. I was honestly hoping that today would be much more mellow.

I staggered out of the office to find Aunt Thelma fresh as a summer daisy behind the front counter.

"Morning, sleepyhead," she said with a smile.

I rubbed my eyes, followed by the middle of my forehead, where I felt the ribbed indentation of the checkbook's metal binding. "Why did you let me sleep in there last night?"

"Well, I did try to wake you, but you swatted me away. I figured you knew where your room was if you wanted to head on up."

I yawned.

"There's fresh coffee if you'd like some." Thelma motioned to the carafe behind the desk where it usually was. Beside it was my favorite black cat mug. The green, glowing eyes and mischievous expression made me smile. I poured myself a piping hot mug full, adding a spoonful of sugar. Strong coffee was just what I needed. I blew on the rim, took a sip, and gagged. ACK!

"What's the matter?" Thelma looked alarmed.

I stuck out my tongue. "What is this?"

And then we heard it, Percy's laughter, as he floated unseen throughout the lobby. "Please tell me it's not poison," I said.

Thelma took the cup from me and sampled it for herself. "Salt," she commented.

"How does he do it?"

"Picked your favorite mug, didn't you?"

I inhaled through my nose, causing my nostrils to flare.

"You haven't changed as much as you think."

I scowled at that thought. Of course, I'd changed. I was not the same naive girl that left this town all those years ago. I'd become someone, and I was well on my way with the credentials to prove it.

"You know what your problem is?"

"A disrespectful ghost?" I replied sarcastically.

"You need to lighten up. You take life too seriously."

"Life is serious."

"Only if you let it be."

I ignored my aunt and looked down at my ruined coffee. "I'm going to get that ghost yet." I sulked off to the small kitchen on the first floor and dumped my coffee down the drain, rinsing the mug out in the process. When I refilled it the second time, I used sugar packets just to be safe.

While I doctored up my coffee, Aunt Thelma took a phone call. I inadvertently eavesdropped. It was Clemmie, and she was worried about how slow business had been from the sounds of it. I hadn't given it much thought as I rode through town yesterday, probably because my mind was elsewhere, but Clemmie was right. The town did look sleepy. I could've parked right up front at Village Square if I had wanted to. Plenty of spots were open, which didn't bode well for business.

"It's not just you, dear," Aunt Thelma said to her friend. "Diane's been worried too."

I sipped my coffee while listening, and an idea came to mind. While Thelma and Clemmie brainstormed how to bring Silverlake to the future, I thought maybe it should stay in the past. By the time the ladies ended their conversation, I had a plan.

"What if you didn't try to change Silverlake?" I said.

"What do you mean?"

"Silverlake is full of old-world charm, and the classic family vacations that people used to love can still be found here—only with the modern amenities of today. Instead of trying to be something you're not, cater to what you are. Fill the void people are missing in their lives. Believe me, out there, life moves at warp speed." I held up my cell phone for emphasis. Even with spotty reception, I still had dozens of emails, texts, and social media notifications clamoring for my attention. "People need a break from all that noise, witches included."

"What about you?" Aunt Thelma smiled at me knowingly.

"No, not me. Just everyone else." And then I laughed. Even I had to admit how ridiculous I sounded. "Anyway, we need to spruce things up a bit here and then host an event that will really bring tourists down."

"Sooner rather than later," Thelma quipped.

"Before Silverlake becomes a ghost town." I finished my aunt's sentence.

"Hey now!" Percy objected from somewhere unseen.

"Oh, like you're offended," I shot back.

"What did you have in mind?" my aunt asked me.

I looked off into the distance. If I was running the hotel, what would I do? What would get witches excited? I remembered all the fun I'd had as a kid running around Silverlake and how magical it all felt, especially when the evenings grew shorter and the weather cooler, which would be relatively soon. I glanced down at the calendar on the desk. "What if we hosted a fall festival? It would take a lot of work, and all the businesses would have to come together, but it could be great." I ran with the ideas as they came to me. "We could offer hayrides around Village Square, a pumpkin-carving contest, cider and donuts for sale, maybe even a corn roast, or other food vendors. Ooh! We could cap everything off with a harvest moon dance. Set up a bandstand in Wishing Well Park, string up white lights in the trees. Can you picture it? It would be beautiful. If we were in Chicago, I'd know the perfect band to call."

Excitement bubbled within me. I felt all tingly like I did whenever I planned a new event. I could picture the town's decorations, like the jack-o'-lanterns that could light the drive into the village. "Plus, with witches, fall already is magical. We should capitalize on that."

"You're right. I'm going to call the village council

now and see if we can round up a meeting this afternoon."

"Good idea. I'm going to grab a notebook and start jotting some thoughts down."

While Aunt Thelma made her phone calls, I disappeared upstairs to the third floor where the private apartments were.

I had spent only two seconds in my bedroom the day before, just enough time to deposit my luggage. Looking at the room now, though, I saw that it, too, was left untouched. Even my jewelry box was in the same spot. I swallowed hard, not feeling brave enough to open it and take a trip down memory lane. The closet was in a similar state—full of clothes that had long since gone out of fashion.

"I can't believe she held on to everything all this time," I said to the empty room. I figured Aunt Thelma would have boxed it up and donated it to charity years ago. I should do that before I leave.

Showered and refreshed—well, as much as one can be when they spend the night sleeping with their head on a desk—I headed back downstairs and searched for some breakfast. The few guests staying at the hotel were taking their morning meal outside on the patio, overlooking the lake. Swans floated past. I debated taking my breakfast out and enjoying the last bit of the sunrise when I reminded myself that this wasn't a vacation. I had plenty of work to do and even more so if the town guardians decided to go through with my festival plans.

"Where's Martha?" I asked my aunt in the back kitchen as she readied a platter of fruit and danish pastries to set out for the guests. That was a task the inn's cook always managed.

"Martha? Oh, honey, she passed away years ago."

"What? I didn't know that."

"I called. You didn't answer." My aunt gave me a sympathetic smile and walked out with a platter in each hand.

I nodded and swallowed hard, but the guilt was still lodged in my throat. With nothing else to do, I took a bowl of fruit and a second cup of coffee back to the office. Setting down my breakfast, I went over to the window and pulled the blind up to open it. Or rather, that was what I attempted to do. If Aunt Thelma hadn't opened the door in years, she certainly hadn't bothered with the windows.

"Oh, let me get that for you, dear." Aunt Thelma pulled her wand out from her pocket and pointed it at the window. "Anoxie," she said, and the window lifted on its own. A soft breeze filtered in, and the room immediately felt less stuffy.

"Where is your wand?" Aunt Thelma asked.

"My wand?"

"Surely, you still carry a wand."

I gave my aunt a look that said, "'fraid not."

"Well, your old one is still upstairs in your room.

Nightstand drawer, I believe." Aunt Thelma turned to leave but then stopped and spoke over her shoulder. "A witch should never be without her wand, Angelica. You know that."

That was true if I was still a witch, and I didn't have the heart to tell Aunt Thelma that I wasn't.

CHAPTER FOUR

The bookstore was shaped like a piece of pie—narrow in the front and curved wide in the back. Shoppers could enter from either side. My favorite was the back entrance. Two factory-sized windows flanked the back door. With their twenty-four panes of glass each, the four-by-six windows let in a plethora of sunshine and ample reading light. Outside was a rear patio with wrought iron tables and chairs set up. Of course, they weren't as comfortable as the plush lounge chairs found inside, but you could run next door to the cafe for an iced coffee or a quick lunch and sit outside with a good book for hours. The cafe's outdoor patio was positioned out front, making the back of the bookstore peaceful, especially with the lovely garden blooms and the trickling garden fountain.

The meeting was taking place upstairs on the second floor. It was the area with the most open floor space and where authors often did readings or held talks and workshops on various topics. I eyed the dessert table that Diane, the bakery owner, had set up. Lemon tartlets, miniature double chocolate cupcakes, and frosted sugar cookies looked tempting, but maybe I'd wait until after the meeting. I needed to stay in business mode. Seeing so many faces from my past rattled my nerves, including the owner of the cafe.

"Angelica, I heard a rumor you were in town," the woman said with a warm smile.

"Mrs. Blackwell," I stammered.

"Oh, call me Heather."

"Right." Heather. At one time, I was going to call her mom, as in mother-in-law. I exhaled.

"This was all your idea?" Heather motioned to the packed room.

"It was."

"I like it."

I smiled in response as I took in the room.

I recognized Craig Daniels, the tavern owner, Lyle Peters, the jeweler, and ... "Is that Misty?"

"Hm? Oh, yeah. She took over the bookstore after Mrs. Hawethorn retired."

Misty waved, noticing me, and I waved back with a smile. I was happy to see my once close friend and tried not to let the guilt creep in from never returning her calls, which eventually stopped altogether.

Yeah, I definitely was feeling nervous now. I began to think that maybe this wasn't such a good idea. I should've laid out the festival plans and let Aunt Thelma run with it. I mean, the mayor wasn't even in town. Wasn't this something we should consult her on? Granted, Mayor Parrish was an opinionated and often difficult woman, but she'd want to be involved. I knew she would. Too bad Aunt Thelma disagreed. She thought it was rather to our benefit that Mayor Parrish was at a spa retreat in Sedona.

As Aunt Thelma called the meeting to order and everyone quieted down, I started wondering what the heck I was doing standing in front of everyone. And then, my conscience reminded me how much I loved my aunt and how absent I'd been. She needed my help. I could run away from my problems, but I couldn't abandon her.

"Heeeello!" Aunt Thelma's voice raised above the crowd. "Thank you all for coming here today, and on such short notice. As you can all see, my darling niece is back in town, and she has a wonderful idea that will help us all. Angelica?" Aunt Thelma turned the meeting over to me rather abruptly.

I cleared my throat, and Lyle, the jeweler, blew his nose rather loudly. The jeweler had an awful-sounding cold. "Yes, right." I pulled my shirt taut and took my spot behind the lectern. "I heard a rumor that business has been slow lately. Not at all what's expected this time of year."

Several heads nodded in agreement. Lyle sneezed again.

"That got me thinking about how we could change that, and I came up with an idea. I propose the town host a fall festival. We could offer hayrides, a pumpkin-carving contest, a fall dessert bake-off, food, games ... you name it. We could even cap the whole event off with a community dance at Wishing Well Park. Each shop could sponsor an activity or an event, and if we promote it right, I think we can draw in some big crowds."

I stopped talking to gauge people's reactions. Misty gave me a thumbs up in the back, but not everyone agreed with her.

"Why wait until the fall?" asked Lyle, his voice nasally. "Our businesses are hurting now."

"Well, planning events of this size takes time," I rationalized.

"We don't have time," Lyle said before sneezing once more.

"Trust me. You don't want to rush this. It's no good planning a big event if people don't know about it or have time to get here."

"What do you know about this town? You haven't been here in years," Lyle snapped.

I felt my face flush. "That's true, but I know tourism and what it takes to plan events. It's what I do in Chicago."

"Silverlake isn't Chicago," Lyle retorted.

"I know that—" Lyle cut me off, and I was visibly annoyed.

"And if we wait much longer, I don't know how many of us will still be in business." Lyle looked around the group but failed to find the support he was looking for.

"It might just be your business in the toilet," Craig, the tavern owner, said in a gruff voice.

"Says the town drunk," Lyle retorted.

"What did you say?" Craig, who had been leaning against the bookshelf with his arms folded across his chest, stood and took two steps toward Lyle.

"Now, now," Aunt Thelma said. "Fall is but a few weeks away. We're already in August. We could pick an early September date if everyone agrees?"

I opened my mouth to object, thinking an October date would be even better, but saw how many people liked Aunt Thelma's suggestion. I guess time was of the essence and more critical than I had realized.

"The first weekend of September then." Aunt Thelma pulled out her cell phone and scrolled until she found what she was looking for. "September 7th work for everyone?" she asked, holding up the calendar on her phone.

I mentally calculated how many days that was away and wasn't happy with the results. I wasn't sure if it was enough time to get people here. I'd have to start actively marketing this thing today.

"Great, it's settled. Now, who would like to be on the committee with Angelica?"

At that comment, I did object. "I can just give you guys my notes and let you take it from there."

"Nonsense. This festival was your idea, and we're not going to take that away from you. We know you love Silverlake as much as we do, and there's no one better, or more qualified, to bring this vision to reality than you." Aunt Thelma winked. She knew I wouldn't contradict her praise in front of the town. I replied with a tight-lipped smile.

When it was all said and done, a small committee had formed, including me, Misty (the bookstore owner), Diane (the baker), and Roger (the florist). I suggested we meet the following morning at La Luna, Diane's bakery. But, the team was eager to get to work immediately, so we decided to have a lunch meeting next door at the cafe after cleaning up the bookstore.

With the town meeting officially adjourned and myriad tasks for me to tackle, I sidestepped the small talk and walked over to the dessert table. I had already finished one of the cupcakes and nabbed my second choice, a sugar cookie in the shape of a star, when a downstairs argument reached my ears. Everyone else around me seemed to be too caught up in their conversations to pick up on it.

I nibbled on the sugar cookie and followed the voices. Peering over the balcony to the ground floor, I heard Craig and Lyle arguing just out of sight.

"Town drunk? You've got some nerve. I should go

back upstairs and tell everyone what type of man you really are."

"Are you threatening me?" Lyle asked.

"If divulging your true character is a threat, then I guess I am."

"Pay up," the voice said behind me.

I jumped and turned around. Misty was standing there with her palm outstretched. "Jumpy much?" she gazed downstairs, but the men were no longer visibly.

"Hm?"

"What's going on?"

"Oh, nothing. What were you saying?"

"I was just coming to cash in on that bet."

"What bet?" I asked.

"The one where you said you were never coming back. How'd your aunt do it?" Misty asked.

"She told me she was dying."

That got a laugh out of Misty. "Nice. I should've thought of that sooner."

"You look like you're doing well with the bookstore."

"I like it. The opportunity fell in my lap, and I scooped it up. You got to take a risk now and then, you know?" I nodded politely even though I couldn't disagree more. "I'm just thankful that Mrs. Hawethorn is letting me purchase everything on a land contract. I'm giving her a portion of the sales until it's paid off, which may take longer than I was expecting." Misty didn't seem pleased about that.

"Business has been that bad, huh?"

"I don't know what it is, people just quit coming, and we've all just sat around waiting for things to get better."

"I'm surprised Mayor Parrish or the town council didn't come up with a plan before now."

Misty rolled her eyes. "They're useless. I think they just like to meet at Diane's once a month and eat donuts."

"That's awful."

"It is. I love this town. Others say they do, but they sure don't act like it."

I nodded, feeling like there was more to Misty's comment but not wanting to get into it.

"Don't you miss it?" Misty asked.

"Miss what?"

"The magic."

Before I could answer, Aunt Thelma joined our conversation. "Well, I know I could never live without it, but you know Angelica. She'd rather have her nose in a book than a wand in her hand."

"Excuse me, standing right here," I replied.

Aunt Thelma continued, "What did you say about magic? It wasn't what?" She turned the question to me.

"Practical," I answered, remembering the conversation my aunt and I had the night before I left.

"Not practical? What? You know better than that," Misty replied.

I looked at my friend and shook my head, suggesting otherwise.

"You're telling me that you haven't cast a spell since you left?" Misty asked.

"I don't even own a wand," I confessed.

"Technically, you do." Aunt Thelma held up her index finger to make a point. "It's upstairs in your room," she reminded me for the second time.

"Where it shall remain," I added.

"I think life would be rather dull without magic," Misty said.

"And I agree," Aunt Thelma said.

"Well, I think my life is just fine," I said.

"But why be just fine," Misty said, using air quotes, "when your life can be enchanted?" Misty pulled her wand out from her pocket and waved it. A cupcake appeared in her hand.

I smiled at the display but knew how conjuring worked. Things didn't just appear out of thin air, but rather they were summoned from somewhere else. If you conjured a thousand bucks, you could bet it was coming out of someone else's pocket, which was why conjuring cash was illegal to do.

"Or you could walk five steps and pick up a cupcake off the dessert table," I remarked, pointing to where the cupcake had originated from.

A loud booming sneeze punctuated the air. Lyle may have been on the small size, but his cold wasn't. He shuffled his feet up the stairs, looking rather miserable.

"Well, how about this for practicality." Aunt Thelma pulled her wand out from her purse and pointed it at Lyle. She mumbled an incantation, and a green streak shot out of her wand. I jumped back at the display of power.

Lyle froze when the spell hit him in the chest. He stood in suspended animation and then fell right over, lying dead as a doornail.

A gasp rippled through the crowd.

"Quick, call 911!" I shouted. Everyone looked at me like I had lost my mind. I forgot that the town still only had an operator. If you wanted the sheriff, fire department, or an ambulance, you had to dial zero. Silverlake wasn't big enough for a central dispatch, and a regular police officer or ambulance couldn't enter.

I raced forward as Aunt Thelma stood motionless in shock. Roger met me over Lyle's body.

"He's dead," Roger announced, checking for a pulse.

"What did you do?" I snapped at Aunt Thelma before realizing the implication of my words.

"Me? Nothing! I just cast a little spell to clear up his cold. I certainly didn't kill him."

In no time, the sheriff's department arrived, and I was grateful to see them. Out of the twenty or so of us present, no one seemed to know what to do as shock set in. We were all in denial. Surely Lyle Peters wasn't dead. He must just have passed out. Except for the lack of a pulse. That I couldn't explain. We were downstairs, giving the first responders space to work. As the minutes ticked by, Aunt Thelma's complexion paled.

"You're sure you didn't kill him?" I asked my aunt. We were standing in the cooking section. Over her shoulder, I read the spine of a rather large volume—Potions for Potlucks. I could only imagine what the recipes entailed.

"Heavens no. It was a spell I've used hundreds of times. Anytime I feel the slightest sniffle coming on, I use it. But," Aunt Thelma's voice trailed off.

"But what?" I whispered.

Aunt Thelma shook her head, and I knew this wasn't the best place to be having this conversation. I led her down the narrow passageway through the back seating area and right out the door. Goldfinches fluttered about, and the fountain bubbled peacefully in the background. Nature seemed to not have a care in the world. "But what?" I repeated.

"It's just an awful coincidence, isn't it?"

"It is. Could your spell have set something off?"

"Like what?" Aunt Thelma asked in disbelief.

"I don't know. Could it have counteracted another spell already in his system?" I threw out hopefully.

"You know magic doesn't work that way. It's not like taking too much cold medicine."

I sighed, unsure of what to make of it.

"Well, well, well. Look who we have out here," A blonde bombshell in a deputy uniform said to us as she walked out the back door. "Come out here to get your story straight?"

"Amber?" I stared back at the one person who I had

despised in high school.

"That's Deputy Reynolds to you," she said as she eyed up what I was wore.

"I thought your father was the deputy," I replied, trying not to feel self-conscious as she stared me up and down.

"He's sheriff now." Amber smacked her gum in tight bubbles against her tongue.

"Oh, nice," I said, even though I didn't mean it. Amber's father was the type of deputy who liked to hide in his cruiser behind the bank ATM on the other side of the lake and pull over anyone who went two miles over the speed limit. Heaven help you if you ran the town's singular stoplight, conveniently also by the bank. I could only imagine the type of sheriff he was.

"So what are you two doing? Trying to sneak away?" Amber eyed us suspiciously.

"What? Oh, no. I was ... I mean, we were just stepping outside to get some air." I had to admit, the two of us did look rather guilty standing outside whispering.

"And hide the murder weapon?" Amber raised her eyebrows.

"What are you talking about?" I asked.

"Your wand, Thelma. Hand it over."

"I'll do no such thing." Aunt Thelma looked defiant.

"I've got more than one witness accusing you of cursing Lyle to death."

"I did not. The poor man had a cold, so I did a quick healing spell to make him feel better."

"Are you a licensed healer?" Amber knew darn well that Aunt Thelma wasn't.

"This is ridiculous. Where is my wand? I'll show you. I'll do the spell on myself." Aunt Thelma looked around for her wand, patting her capri pants pockets and coming up empty. "Oh, where is the darn thing? I keep losing it. First, it was at Roger's, and then at the bakery. By the time I got home, I couldn't find it anywhere. Thankfully, Lyle lent me his," Aunt Thelma continued to ramble.

"Wait, that was Lyle's wand you killed him with?" Amber asked.

"I didn't kill him! I was trying to cure him!" Aunt Thelma exclaimed.

"Where's your purse?" I asked, remembering where her wand was last.

"Oh, that's right. That's where it was. It's upstairs."

"I'll find it. And then you and the wand are coming with me to the station," Amber demanded.

"I don't think so," Aunt Thelma replied.

"Fine, then I'll have to place you under arrest for the murder of Lyle Peters."

"You wouldn't!" Aunt Thelma placed her hand on her heart.

"I would be well within my rights," Amber replied coolly.

"Well, I suppose when you put it that way. Can you please go grab my purse? And I'll be happy to pop in at the station for a quick chat."

"'That's more like it. You two, don't move. I'll be back in one minute." Amber watched us all the way to the door. "Jones, keep an eye on them," she said to the other uniformed officer.

I looked at Aunt Thelma out of the corner of my eye, wondering if she was going to make a break for it.

"Now, don't look at me that way. I'm sure everything will be fine. I'll go down to the station, answer a few quick questions, and be on my merry little way."

I wanted to believe Aunt Thelma, but I had a sinking suspicion that her chat would be anything but quick. My cell phone rang in my pocket. I glanced at it. It was Lacey. I'd have to call her back later.

Amber came back shortly with Aunt Thelma's purse but no wand.

"I swear, we don't have it," I said, but that didn't stop the deputy from patting us down. She wasn't happy when she came up empty-handed.

"Jones, section off the bushes and start looking for a wand," she instructed. "Thelma, come with me. Angelica, I expect you to stay in town."

"Of course," I said with attitude. I really didn't like that woman.

Amber led Aunt Thelma down the stone path toward the store's front when I thought of something.

"What if he was poisoned?" I offered up, remembering the dessert table. Amber stopped walking and seemed to be listening. "There's a whole selection of goodies upstairs. Lyle could've eaten something that was tainted."

"Did you see him eat anything?" Amber asked.

"Well, no. But that doesn't mean he didn't."

"Did you see anyone else eat anything?" Amber questioned further.

"Well, yeah. I did. Misty did," I said, remembering the conjured cupcake. "I'm positive other people did too. The table was pretty well picked over after the meeting."

"And did anyone else drop dead?"

I glared at Amber, not dignifying her question with a response.

"All I'm saying is it's possible that he, and only he, was poisoned."

"So now you think it was premeditated?" Amber looked incredulous.

"It could've been. I mean, I heard Lyle and Craig arguing just before he died."

"The tavern owner?" Amber asked for clarification.

"Mm-hm. That's him. They got into it downstairs."

"Really? Well, some might say that you argued with Lyle as well." Amber's voice was eerily calm.

"I did not." But then I snapped my mouth shut, remembering the back-and-forth between Lyle and me at the meeting.

"If I were you, Angelica, I'd be careful with what you say and who you accuse," Amber warned. I kept my mouth closed and let her lead my aunt away.

CHAPTER FIVE

News of Lyle's death quickly spread through the town. A crowd had gathered by the time Amber escorted Aunt Thelma to her car.

"You guys go ahead with the meeting. This won't take long," Aunt Thelma assured me once more before getting in the car.

"What in the heavens is going on?"

I turned to find Clemmie standing beside me.

"Where have you been?" I said to my aunt's best friend. My original plan to give Clemmie a piece of my mind slipped away.

"Bridal shower. Full house. I couldn't get away." Clemmie ran the tea shop one street over from the bookstore, making it a quick walk.

"Aunt Thelma's been arrested for cursing Lyle Peters to death." I shook my head in disbelief even as I said the words.

"Why would she go and do that? We all know Lyle's a pain in the butt, but it's not like Thelma to go off killing somebody just for a character flaw."

"She didn't really kill him. At least I don't think so." I relayed to Clemmie what had happened. "Which is why Amber's taking her down to the station for questioning."

"Except she can't find the wand." Misty joined our group. "Amber has Deputy Jones searching for it upstairs." I tried to think back to the seconds following Lyle hitting the ground, and I couldn't remember what Aunt Thelma had done with the wand. She must've dropped it. That's the only explanation I could think of if it wasn't upstairs in her purse.

"And she shut my business down as a crime scene." Misty didn't bother hiding the frustration in her voice.

"Now, what do we do?" I asked the group, which now consisted of Clemmie, Misty, Diane, and Roger.

"First things first, we need to call Boyd. See if he'll meet Thelma down at the station and represent her. I don't trust Amber or her father one bit," Clemmie said.

"She'll have Thelma locked up for life before the weekend," Diane said.

"Mm-hm. You know it," Clemmie said.

"Boyd's still practicing? I thought he retired." When I interned with him in high school, Boyd Andrews had been in his fifties, or maybe I just thought he was. I'd never been a good judge of age.

"Ha, I don't think he knows the word. I wouldn't be

surprised if Boyd worked until the day he died," Clemmie remarked.

"Well, I'm not so sure about that," Diane added. "I think he's settling down a bit."

"As long as he's practicing law today, that's all that matters," Roger chimed in.

"I agree." I took out my cell phone and started to look up Boyd's office number, but Clemmie rattled off the digits. I punched the numbers in and waited for our lines to connect.

"Silverlake Legal, how may I help you?" the receptionist asked.

"Hi, this is Angela, I mean, Angelica Nightingale." I made sure to use my full name to help Boyd recognize me. "Is Mr. Andrews by chance available?"

"He thought you might call. Hold, please."

"Thank you." I covered the phone with my hand. "I guess he's expecting my call," I said to the group.

"Angelica? Is that you? I heard you were in town. Although, I'm betting this isn't a social call."

"Have you heard about Lyle Peters?" I asked.

"I sure did." Boyd's words hung in the air as if he was going to add to the sentence. Eventually, he said, "How's your aunt?"

"Well, Amber Reynolds just took her in for questioning. I was hoping you could meet them at the station. I don't like the idea of her interrogating my aunt without legal representation."

"No, I agree. Thelma should have a lawyer present, but I'm afraid I can't do it."

"What?" That wasn't the answer I was expecting. "Why not?"

"It's a conflict of interest."

"What do you mean?"

"I'm afraid that's all I can say. But you're right. Your aunt does need a lawyer and a good one. Would you like a referral?"

"Uh, sure."

"I'll have Cindy give you the number. Hold on a minute."

"Okay, thanks." I relayed to the group what was going on.

"Conflict of interest? What's that all about?" Clemmie asked.

"He must be representing Lyle on a different matter," Roger remarked.

"I can believe that, seeing he's one of the only lawyers in town," said Diane.

I barely heard the rest of the conversation as I was waiting for Cindy to pick up the line, but after a couple of minutes of silence, the call hung up. "Well, then," I said to the phone.

"Let's head next door to the cafe and regroup. We're getting an awful lot of lookee loos out here," Clemmie suggested.

I looked up from my phone and noticed she was

right. People were side-eyeing us and whispering. I felt uncomfortable right down to the tips of my toes. "You're right. Let's go."

"I'll meet you guys shortly. I'm going to hang over here for a minute and see if they need me for anything," Misty said.

"Okay, sounds good," I said, not wanting to stand outside a moment longer.

I DIDN'T FEEL like eating, but Heather insisted, bringing out my favorite, her homemade Monte Cristo sandwich with powdered sugar dusted on top and sweet raspberry jam on the side. She served it with seasoned fries and a large peach iced tea.

"Eat. It'll help you think," Heather said with a wink.

I was about to ask the group who else was a decent lawyer in town when one walked right in the door. I stared at my ex-boyfriend and about choked. Something that sounded like a combination of a gargle and a gasp came out of my mouth. I coughed hard. Clemmie gave me a wallop on the back and handed me a napkin. I swiped it from her hand and blotted my face.

Words failed me. Tall, blond, blue eyes ... Vance had nearly been the death of me. The man looked as handsome as ever even in his athletic wear. Thankfully, Vance didn't notice me—or my visceral reaction. He walked right up to his mom, kissed her on the cheek, and sat down at the lunch counter next to an older man. The two began chatting as small-town locals do.

I cleared my throat and tried to regain my composure, ignoring the fact that Clemmie was snickering. I wouldn't let Vance phase me. I was surprised, that's all. No one told me he was back in town. Instead, I gave myself a pep talk while taking a long drag of iced tea. You're a mature, successful woman. You're not going to let something silly like a high school romance throw you off your game. Except ... he was your first love and the reason you left town. I squeezed my eyes shut as a brain freeze hit and set my glass down. There were too many memories in Silverlake, which is exactly why I left. Chicago had given me the fresh start I needed.

Before I could find my voice or a way to stop Clemmie, she was up, power-walking across the cafe and tapping Vance on his shoulder. Within seconds, he turned and looked over and caught my eye. My tummy did a little flip-flop, and I offered a lame wave in response.

Mature, confident woman, I repeated, willing myself to act like it. The last time Vance and I spoke, the words hadn't been nice. Things hadn't ended on good terms, and I didn't think I'd ever talk to him again, not if I could help it, and yet here he was, walking over to the table.

"I should snap a picture. The big reunion," Heather

commented with a smile while serving a piece of pie one table over. I couldn't help the glare I shot her.

"What's this about your aunt?" Vance asked me.

"Hi, Vance, nice to see you, too," I replied.

"I told you, she's been arrested. You need to take her case and head on down to the station," Clemmie said, ignoring the tension between Vance and me.

"Technically, Amber just took her in for questioning. I don't think she's been arrested," I said.

"Whatever. We need your help," Clemmie said.

"Tell me what happened," Vance asked.

I left it to Clemmie to fill him in.

She was in the middle of talking when I interrupted. "Weren't you practicing estate law down in Florida?"

"Oh no, Vance has been back here for what, two years?" Diane estimated.

"About that. Estate law didn't last long. I made a career out of criminal defense, and a couple of years ago, I decided I missed home." Vance looked at me, and I nodded without another word.

"And I've been happy to have my baby home ever since," Heather stopped by and kissed her son on the cheek, a dirty plate in each hand.

"So, what do you say? Will you take the case?" Clemmie asked Vance.

"I mean, yeah, if that's okay with you, Angie." Vance looked to me for approval.

What was I supposed to say? No? Aunt Thelma

needed a lawyer, Boyd wasn't available, and one was standing in front of me offering up his services. My hands were tied.

"Yeah, of course," I replied with more enthusiasm than I felt.

Clemmie clapped her hands together. "All right then. I guess you better scoot while the rest of us get to work."

Vance raised his eyebrows.

"Fall festival. Angelica's idea," Roger supplied.

"Right." It was my idea, wasn't it?

"I'll leave you guys to it, and I'll call you," Vance said, pointing to me, "once I know something."

"Sure, sounds good." Heather walked by and handed me a pen from her waitress apron. I took it, all the while repeating "mature, confident woman" in my head. I scribbled my cell phone number down on the white, square napkin and handed it to Vance.

With Vance heading down to the sheriff's department, I thought I would focus on the task at hand, but my head wasn't in planning mode.

"Does anyone know what Lyle did today, before the meeting?" I asked while we finished our lunches. My appetite was surprisingly back in full force.

"I saw him stop and get breakfast at your place, didn't he, Diane?" Roger asked.

"What?" Diane looked up. Her mind was off wandering.

"Didn't Lyle stop in at your place this morning for breakfast?" Roger asked again.

"Oh, not that I know of. But, I was working in the back. I suppose he could've stopped in, and I didn't know about it," Diane remarked.

"And I could be mistaken about seeing him there," Roger said. "My memory's not quite what it used to be."

"Except when it comes to knowing all those flower names," Clemmie said.

"This is true. I do love zantedeschia aethiopica," Roger said with a smile.

"Which is ..." I let my question trail off.

"Calla lilies," Roger supplied.

"A favorite of mine as well," Diane remarked.

They were mine too. I had always envisioned having a bunch of white calla lilies tied with a ribbon for a wedding bouquet. I hadn't thought about that for years, and I kept the memory to myself, even now.

"So, Lyle may or may not have stopped by the bakery," I said.

"I don't know if he stopped in the bakery, but I saw him this morning at the bank," Heather said while stopping by to refill our glasses with a pitcher of iced tea.

"You did?" I asked as I pushed my glass forward. Heather's peach tea was addictive.

"Yes, ma'am. He was meeting with Mr. Barker, the manager," Heather said.

"Well, he did say he might not be in business if we waited too long for the festival," Roger pointed out.

"That's true," I said, looking thoughtful.

"What are you thinking?" Clemmie asked.

"I don't know. I guess I'm trying to understand how Lyle could have just died like that."

"Maybe it was a coincidence," Diane suggested, but I don't think any of us believed that.

"What did I miss?" Misty asked, joining our table.

"Angelica is just trying to outline Lyle's morning routine," Clemmie said.

"Didn't he stop by your place for breakfast, Diane?" Misty asked.

Diane threw her hands up in the air. "So everyone tells me. But I didn't see him."

"How's it going next door?" Roger asked.

"It was pointless for me to stay. They won't even let me past the front door. Figured I might as well come over here.

"Thanks for that. We have plenty of work to divvy up. Should we start then?" I asked.

The conversation swung over to the task at hand. Diane offered to be the contact person for the food vendors. Roger was going to check with the town council for permits. Misty was going to talk to local store owners about donating raffle items, which left me to coordinate the community activities like the pumpkin-carving contest and harvest moon dance. Hopefully, Mayor Parrish wouldn't create too much of a fuss when she got back in town. I wasn't holding my breath. The consensus was to have the ball rolling on as much as possible, making it hard for her to put the kibosh on it. With that business settled and a plan to regroup the following day, our meeting adjourned.

CHAPTER SIX

I was shocked when I got back to the inn and saw Vance dropping Aunt Thelma off.

"Wow, that was fast," I said as I joined the two of them under the hotel awning.

"Speak for yourself. That Amber woman is a nightmare. Her questioning gave me a headache." Aunt Thelma touched the tips of her fingers to her temples.

"She was trying to trip you up," Vance remarked.

Aunt Thelma ignored Vance's comment and said, "If only I had my wand. I know the perfect spell," she said, referencing her headache.

"No! Enough magic for one day," exasperation heavy in my voice. Vance cocked his head toward me but kept his mouth shut. "Start with a couple of Tylenol, and if it's still bothering you in a little bit, we can give Constance a call. She's still a healer, right?"

And had legitimate medical credentials after her name, I should add.

"She is," Vance remarked.

"You're no fun," Aunt Thelma scoffed.

I shot Vance a look that dared him to agree with her. He was wise and kept his mouth shut, which prompted me to say, "You'd think seeing a man die after getting hit with a spell, one that you cast, would make you step away from magic for a bit."

"Why on earth would I do that? I didn't kill him." Aunt Thelma narrowed her eyes. "It would be smart of you to remember that not everything in Silverlake is what it seems. Now you two come inside, I'm parched," she held the inn's door open invitingly and waved us through.

I took a step back. "I think I'll take a walk. I'll catch up with you later." I turned and walked away. Behind me, I heard my aunt say, "My word. What is wrong with that girl?"

I couldn't make out Vance's reply.

I hadn't planned on taking a walk and wasn't dressed for one either, but now that I had stated my intention, I felt compelled to see it through. I walked behind the inn and picked up Enchanted Trail. The walking path wound itself around the lake and behind the village center shops. The trail was nothing more than a foot-worn walkway that the locals had used for years. Eventually, the city council put mulch down, but as I picked up the trail on the other side of the waterfront, I could tell it had been some time since the council put fresh wood chips down.

Walking clockwise past the hotel, I followed the trail as it weaved in front of the campground, where a handful of waterfront cabins were available to rent by the week. Behind them were open lots for tents and campers. The thought of hauling a trailer over that rickety wooden bridge was enough to give me heart palpitations.

Bits of brightly colored nylon fabric from tents and shiny chrome campers were visible through the thick, green foliage. The heavy scent of wood smoke mixed with pine hung in the air. I inhaled deeply. It had been a long time since I had been in the great outdoors. At one time, an avid hiker, I'd given up hitting the trailhead for the steady stream of sidewalk that snaked around downtown Chicago. Eventually, I gave up being outside all together for the predictable comfort of my apartment treadmill. But that smell—it hit my senses and took me back. I shook my head. Everything here jolted a memory and made me feel things. Things I didn't want to remember.

"I need to get back to work," I said to the birds chirping overhead. I was about to turn around and head back toward Mystic Inn when my cell phone rang. It was Lacey again. I had forgotten that she'd called a little bit ago.

"Where have you been?" she asked when I hit answer.

"In the twilight zone," I muttered.

"What?"

"Nevermind. What's up?" I walked forward.

"Are you sitting down?"

"No, I'm out on a walk."

"Really?"

"Don't worry. I'm wondering the same thing. But what's going on?"

"Consumer Tech called. They're thinking of hosting next year's convention in Chicago. They invited us to put in a bid."

"Are you serious?" Consumer Tech was one of the largest technology conventions in the country. "You told them yes, right?"

"Of course. I have the proposal deets in front of me. I'm going to start working on it, and I'll send you over a copy when I'm done."

"Okay, I'll check my email when I get to my room."

Lacey and I continued to talk about work as I walked the trail. I was lost in conversation, looking up at the trees, when a person came out of nowhere, barreling right into my shoulder. It was almost as if they sprang from the ground. The force knocked me back and sent my cell phone flying off into the woods.

"Hey!" I hollered at the man's back. He was wearing athletic shorts and running shoes. A hoodie was pulled over his head despite the heat.

"Excuse me!" I yelled once more, trying to get the jerk to stop and apologize. I jogged a couple steps forward, and that's when it hit me—a stunning spell. The red streak of light raced from the tip of the wand, but I hadn't been fast enough. The spell knocked the wind out of me and left me hunched over, immobilized. I willed myself not to panic and counted down the seconds until I'd be free. I hadn't been hit with a stunning spell since I was a kid playing freeze tag. I'd hated it then, too. Thirty seconds, I told myself. It should only last thirty seconds—a minute tops. I could survive a minute. As long as my attacker didn't come back to finish me off. That thought had my heart knocking wildly in my chest. My palms were sweaty. I was a sitting duck, and there wasn't anything I could do about it. My limbs began to tingle like your foot does when it falls asleep as the spell released its hold. I stood fully upright and sucked in a deep breath. My head whipped from side to side, but no one was there. My stomach hurt like I had taken a sucker punch, and really, I had. Aunt Thelma was right. Not everything in Silverlake was what it appeared to be. And I was way outside of my comfort zone.

Thankfully, Lacey was still on the line. I could hear her voice coming from the scrub brush. "Hello? Angela? Are you there? Are you okay? You're making me nervous. I'm going to call the police."

I picked up the phone and blew the dirt off of it. "Don't. I'm here."

"What in the world happened to you? I'm freaking

out here. I thought a bear attacked you. Wait, do you have bears there?"

I ignored Lacey's question. "Listen, someone ran right into me and then took off."

"What? Are you okay? I'm calling the police."

"No, don't." Not that they'd be able to help if she did. I was still debating if I wanted to report the incident to Silverlake's authorities. "I'm okay, but I'm going to let you go. I'll call you in a little bit." I hung up, not waiting for a response, and took in my surroundings. I was coming up to the residential district. It was the area where most locals called home. I could see the town's one stoplight up the embankment and across the street. The light controlled the two-way traffic driving around the lake and from that coming down the hill, which dead-ended at the water. In addition to housing the neighborhood, the residential district was also home to the Silverlake school district, bank, grocery store, and post office. Did that mean that the man who stunned me was a local? I rubbed my stomach absentmindedly and looked back at the path. I shuddered, feeling exposed and unsafe—a feeling I'd never equated with my hometown. I was kitty-corner from the inn on the other side of the lake, and it would take me an equal amount of time to get back to the inn, no matter which way I went. I had no choice but to continue forward. I was keenly aware of my surroundings—every splash in the water, every bird chirping overhead, every buzzing bee. Then, off in the distance, I heard it. The rhythmic thumping of feet hitting the ground. My breath caught as I recognized the sound. Someone was running toward me. It was a constant drumming as the footsteps grew closer.

He's coming back, I thought. Panic washed over me. I tried to stay calm, but in reality, I was utterly defenseless. I decided to make a break for it. A small patch of trees separated the trail system from the town road, where someone else would hopefully drive by. The embankment was steep on this side of the lake, but I could make it. Branches scratched at my ankles as I ran through the brush over the downed trees and piles of leaves. I prayed I wouldn't step on or scare up a snake. I used my forearms to shield my face as the tree branches grew thick. As I approached the embankment, I realized it was taller than I remembered. I was going to have to crawl up it and quickly. The man was right behind me. I could sense him.

"Angie? What are you doing?" I was clawing my way up toward the road when Vance's voice stopped me. I let go and sat down in the dirt. Relief and embarrassment washed over me in equal parts. My khaki capris were dirt-stained, and I had lost a button on my blouse. I opened my mouth to say something witty or sarcastic, but nothing came to mind. The truth was, my heart was racing, and moments ago, I was scared for my life.

Vance must've sensed that. He took out his wand from the waistband of his shorts. Unlike the man who had run into me, Vance was wearing dark blue running shorts with neon green mesh. It was the same color combination that matched his shoes. Why in the world I was noticing that was beyond me. It must be the adrenaline.

I decided to give honesty a try. "Someone knocked into me, sent my cell phone flying. When I hollered after him, he hit me with a stunning spell. I heard running and thought he was coming back for me." I huffed, out of breath, and willed myself not to cry.

"Which way did they go?"

"The way you just came from."

"I didn't see anyone."

"He must've run up the hill to the residential district. There's no point chasing after him now." Vance had a look in his eyes that suggested otherwise. "Please, I just want to get back and get cleaned up." And forget this whole afternoon ever happened.

Vance took one final look through the woods toward the road and relented. "Fine, but I'm walking back with you, and I don't want to hear you argue with me."

I held up my hands in surrender. Besides, anything that would've come out of my mouth would've been a weak attempt to shoo Vance away. I would never admit it out loud, but I was thankful to have someone walk back with me.

"You know, you really should carry a wand," Vance said.

"Noted." I'd survived thirteen years in Chicago without a wand, but one night in Silverlake, and I was second-guessing my resolve.

We walked on in silence for a minute before curiosity got the best of me. "What happened today at the sheriff's department?"

"Your aunt answered their questions, and then they had to let her go. I pointed out that they couldn't arrest someone for murder until they ruled out natural causes."

"You think that's possible? Lyle died of natural causes?" I tried to keep the hope out of my voice.

"No." Vance deadpanned. I smacked his arm.

"Ow." Vance mockingly rubbed his shoulder.

"Now, what do we do?"

"Now, I need to come up with a better defense for your aunt."

"It doesn't look good, does it?"

"Not when you have two dozen eyewitnesses all claiming Thelma killed him."

"I know, I was there and saw it, and yet I still don't believe it. Aunt Thelma didn't mean to hurt Lyle."

"That doesn't mean that she didn't."

I let Vance's reply hang in the air. He had a point. Aunt Thelma could've accidentally killed Lyle. That is, after all, why you had to have a license to heal.

We walked behind the village shops.

"Business seems to be picking up a bit," Vance remarked.

"Probably because it's Friday."

"Or murder's good for business."

I stopped walking. "What did you say?"

"That murder's good for business? Why?"

I started walking again. "Well, it's just that Lyle mentioned how bad business had been lately. He was adamant that we host the festival as soon as possible to bring in revenue."

"Are you suggesting that someone killed Lyle to drum up business?" Vance looked skeptical.

"I agree, it's a long shot, but it's worth looking into, isn't it?"

"Anything is at this point. I'll see what I can find out."

Fifteen minutes later, I had never been happier to see the Mystic Inn. The sun was hot. I was sweaty and wanted nothing more than to take a cold shower and change out of my dirty clothes.

"Thanks for walking me back," I said as we approached the parking lot.

"Anytime." Vance stopped walking and turned toward me, like he wanted to say something.

I avoided his eyes and picked up my pace. "I'll see you later," I called over my shoulder, putting distance between us. That was after all what he wanted. Distance. Space. Time to figure life out and toss our relationship in the trash in the process.

I was fuming in the thirty seconds it took me to reach the inn's lobby. All this time and I still had issues.

What was wrong with me? I wasn't sure if I was more annoyed with myself or Vance. My mood left me not knowing what to think.

"Not a word," I said, pointing to my aunt behind the registration counter as I walked past her inside.

"I didn't say anything," Aunt Thelma murmured.

"You were thinking it," I quipped as I took the stairs to the third floor. Aunt Thelma chuckled behind me.

CHAPTER SEVEN

After getting washed up, I decided it was time to smarten up and level the playing field. I wasn't going to get caught without a wand again. Not here, where no place felt safe. I took my old wand out of the nightstand and tucked it in my purse. Not that I knew what to do with it anymore. At this point, I was better off poking someone's eye with it as opposed to casting any spell, but it was a start.

With trembling fingers, I moved on to my jewelry box. My mother's tiger's eye necklace was right where I'd left it. The circular pendant housed a round, spinning gemstone that dangled on a gold chain. The stone provided protection, courage, strength—and something extra magical. It gave me, and only me, the power to transform into a cat. I clasped the necklace around my neck and looked in the mirror, barely recognizing the woman I'd become. The stone glowed warmly against my chest. I whispered an apology to my mom for leaving it behind. Regardless if I was still a witch or not, it was wrong of me to abandon it.

Back outside, I took the rental car and drove over to the residential district, all the while keeping my eyes peeled for a man wearing athletic shorts and a hoodie, although in my heart, I knew he was no longer lurking around.

As I headed to the bank, Vance's words rattled around in my head: he needed to come up with a better defense for Aunt Thelma. In my mind, that meant identifying who the real killer was. I parked in one of the angled parking spots in front of the community bank and grabbed my purse. Thankfully, there wasn't an ATM out front, making it easier to provide me with a cover.

Walking into the lobby, I stopped short, recognizing Molly McCormick, the greenhouse manager's daughter, working behind the counter as a teller.

"I was hoping I would see you!" Molly came around the counter and wrapped me in a big hug, pinning my arms down at my side. The girl always was a hugger. "Oh my goodness, it's been way too long. I'm so glad you're here!"

"Just for a visit," I added.

"Well, then, I'm happy I got to see you."

"There's not an ATM around here, is there?"

"Village Square has one, although it only works half the time. The council is supposed to replace it, but who knows when." Molly leaned forward and whispered, "Personally, I think Mr. Barker was tired of going over there every other day to fill it." She motioned with her eyes to the manager's office.

"Got it. Can you cash a personal check for me then?"

"Of course, I'd be happy to."

I retrieved my checkbook from my purse and made a check out to cash for one hundred dollars.

"Do you guys do business loans here?" I asked.

Molly nodded while typing on her keyboard. I could tell she was multitasking, and I didn't want to distract her as she opened her drawer and began counting out cash, but she managed to do both simultaneously.

"You have to see Mr. Barker for that. Are you thinking about opening up a new shop in town? There's plenty of retail spaces open." Molly seemed depressed by that.

"Actually, I was thinking about updating the inn. Keeping the historic charm, but modernizing the amenities," or maybe it was the necessities like the ice maker and air-conditioning.

"Well, he's with another customer right now, but I can give you an application. Does that help?"

"That'd be great." Molly counted the cash back to me and then opened another drawer to retrieve the application. She put the paperwork in a folder with the bank's logo on the front and handed it across the counter. It wasn't in my nature to openly gossip, but I took a stab at it and asked Molly if she heard about Lyle.

"Oh my goodness, it's the saddest thing ever, isn't it? I heard they brought your aunt in for questioning too." Molly held up her hand in a stop motion. "I wasn't going to say anything unless you brought it up. I didn't think you'd want to talk about it."

"Thanks, I'm just trying to make sense of it. I heard Lyle was here this morning. Did you wait on him?"

"I did. He asked about a business loan too, come to think of it. Mr. Barker was free, so I sent Lyle to talk with him."

"Got it." It looked like I really needed to talk to the bank manager. Maybe I could when returning these loan papers. The business loan had been a ruse, but money to spruce up the inn was a good idea.

"And I'm sorry about your aunt. For what it's worth, I think she's innocent."

"I do too, and thanks." I took my cash and the loan application and walked out of the bank. I sat in the car and thought for a moment. The only thing I knew about Lyle was that he had a cold, and his business needed money. Nothing that wasn't common knowledge or would help Aunt Thelma. I hoped I could uncover more, and soon because time was not on my side.

INSTEAD OF GOING BACK to the inn, I decided to stop by the tavern under the pretense of securing raffle donations. Hopefully, Misty hadn't beat me to it. I wasn't sure if Craig would talk to me, but I hoped to uncover the backstory between his and Lyle's argument. The tavern was next door to the jewelry store, and I wondered if that wasn't at the heart of their disagreement.

Despite business being slow, the bar was full of witches looking to grab a hot meal and a cold beer. The interior was decorated with dark woods and warm leather on the barstools and the backs of booths. The bar itself was mahogany with brass accents. Dragon artwork in the form of paintings and sketches decorated the walls. The floor was red brick, and the lighting soft yellow as it filtered through the overhead mosaic lampshades.

I took a seat at the far end barstool.

"What can I get for you?" an older woman named Bonnie asked me. Her silver-streaked hair was pulled back in a messy bun, and her skin was tan like someone who spent an awful lot of time out in the sun. "I'll be right with you," she said to a man who sat down a couple of barstools from me.

"You always keep me waiting, Bonnie," the man joked back.

Bonnie replied with a husky laugh. "And yet you keep coming back." She turned back to me with her eyebrows raised.

"I was just wondering if Craig was available?" I asked.

"He's not, but I'm his better half. What can I do for you?"

"Oh, sorry. I am Angelica Nightingale. I'm helping organize the fall festival. I wasn't sure if Misty stopped by yet or not, but I was wondering if you guys were interested in donating something for the raffle."

"Oh, yeah. Craig mentioned something about that. Hang on. I think he wrote it down in the back."

"Okay, sounds good." I looked around the bar while waiting for Bonnie to return. I turned to the older man and apologized.

"No worries, I have no other place to be." He was silent for a minute before he said, "Nightingale ... are you related to Thelma?"

"She's my aunt."

"She's a sweetheart. Don't tell her I said that, though. She'd probably curse me with warts."

I laughed at that because the man was probably right. I took the man's friendliness as an invitation to dig a little bit deeper into the tavern. I had a feeling Bonnie wasn't going to tell me much. "So, you come here often, then?"

"When I'm thirsty. Or hungry." The man nodded after each sentence. "So, pretty much every day." He smiled.

"Do you know anything about the jeweler next door?"

"Oh, Mr. Cranky Pants. I heard he kicked the bucket today. Not sorry to see that one go." The man covered his mouth. "Guess I shouldn't speak ill of the dead."

"Do you know if he came in here often?"

The man laughed. "Not if he could help it. He only stopped in to give Craig a hard time. Claimed the tavern customers were always parking in his spots. Don't know what he was so upset about. Not like he was ever busy."

Bonnie came out from the kitchen and walked behind the bar. She had a slip of paper in front of her. "How do two fifty-dollar gift certificates sound?"

"That would be great. I'll be sure to let Misty know. Thanks so much."

Bonnie turned away, dismissing me, and I lost my nerve. Without anything else left to do, I hopped down from the barstool and said goodbye to the man beside me.

"Take care, sweetheart."

"You too."

I walked out of the tavern, disappointed that I hadn't uncovered any secrets, when voices reached my ears. They were coming from across the parking lot. It was Amber and Craig, and by his expression, he wasn't too happy. His face was red, and he was shaking his head. I walked toward them, seeing that's where my car was parked.

"You want to know anything else, you can talk to

my lawyer," Craig said, turning and dismissing himself from Amber's presence. He walked right toward me but thankfully veered off at the last second.

"Excuse me," he said, putting his head down and sidestepping.

"Is everything okay?"

"Just peachy," he replied but stopped walking. "Listen, I don't think your aunt killed Lyle, but don't go looking at pointing the finger at me, you hear?"

"I ... I wasn't," I stammered as I fought to find the right words.

"Like I told that dingbat deputy," Craig motioned at Amber. His words got a snicker out of me, which seemed to help calm him down. "Sorry, I don't really care for her," he said in his defense.

"I'm not going to disagree with you there."

"Anyway, like I told that deputy, if she wants to look for a motive, then she better start with his wife."

"Excuse me? Lyle was married?"

"For over twenty years."

"To who?"

"Diane. You know, the woman who owns the bakery," Craig explained when my expression was blank.

I found my voice. "I had no idea."

"They've been separated forever, probably more years than they were married."

"And they never divorced?"

"Lyle was fighting with her over it. Didn't want to give it to her."

"Why?"

Craig grunted. "Knowing Lyle, it had something to do with money. Anyway, I don't know the details. I only overheard them fighting one night when I was taking out the trash."

"And your beef with Lyle?" I wasn't sure if I bought that it was really over parking spots like the man in the bar suggested.

"Not relevant," Craig said and continued to walk back toward the tavern.

And I wasn't sure I bought that either.

CHAPTER EIGHT

M isty had been busy rounding up raffle items. Between her and Lucy, my inbox chimed every five minutes. Once back at the inn, I started organizing the information on a spreadsheet with each business name and the item they were donating. Silverlake business owners were being generous, which would only help draw in visitors.

After that, I worked on the inn's website, starting with the homepage and creating a landing page for the festival. I would have to purchase additional software before we could accept online reservations sooner rather than later. Online bookings were crucial for increasing guests. People were more apt to book a vacation if they didn't have to pick up the phone and talk to someone. Unfortunately, setting the reservation system up was time-consuming. But that wasn't my biggest challenge. No, my biggest challenge was the guillotine hanging over Aunt Thelma's head. For her part, the woman seemed unfazed, humming along as she restocked the tourist brochures and vacuumed the front rugs. Meanwhile, Percy was busy checking everyone out of the hotel. The few guests we did have were leaving quicker than you could say bibbidi-bobbidi-boo after hearing the proprietor was the number one suspect in a murder.

"Did you find your stay relaxing?" Percy asked with a chuckle as guests deposited their room keys.

"This isn't good," I said as our final guest walked out the door. "What are we going to do?"

"Well, if they give your aunt the chair, she can haunt the place with me." Percy's eyes sparkled at the idea.

"That's not funny!" My face was frozen in horror. I would've smacked the ghost if I could.

"You need to lighten up, Jelly," Percy quipped.

"It's Angelica, and you need to watch your mouth before I cleanse you from this place once and for all."

"Ha! That didn't work before, and it won't work now. I'm a guest. Just ask your aunt."

"We'll see about that," I muttered over my shoulder as I retreated into the office. But just thinking about the amount of work I had to do made my head pound. I didn't have a choice. I was going to have to push through it. Now, more than ever, we needed to upgrade the inn, starting with the reservation system.

An hour later, Aunt Thelma came waltzing into

the office with a duster in hand, something I was positive the woman had never done in the years since I was in Chicago. "What are you working on?" she asked.

"The website," I replied. The sun was setting, dimming the lighting in the office and taking my energy with it. I closed my laptop and sat back for a minute.

"Did you know that Diane was married to Lyle?" I asked.

"Of course. Doesn't everyone?"

"I had no idea," I confessed.

"Oh. Well, it's not a secret, dear."

I tried to think about how to phrase what was on my mind but came up empty.

"Just spit it out. You're obviously thinking something heavy in that head of yours."

"I don't know. Something doesn't sit right with me. I spent most of the afternoon with Diane, and she didn't give off any emotion or even hint at their relationship. She certainly didn't mention they were married."

"Nowadays, it was more of a formality." Aunt Thelma dusted the back desk, something I had done the day before.

"Why didn't they ever get a divorce?"

"I'm not sure. I always assumed it had something to do with their son. You know how families like to stay together when children are involved."

I massaged my temple with my fingers, feeling my headache grow. "Wait, Lyle and Diane have a son?"

"Why, yes, Peter. He owns the wand shop."

"So he's a grown man," which he obviously would be seeing his parents were in their early sixties.

"What did you expect, a baby?"

"But you just said Lyle and Diane stayed married for their son. Don't people usually do that when the kids are young and separate once said children leave the house?"

"Well, they did separate. They just never divorced."

I closed my eyes. Aunt Thelma wasn't following my train of thought. To me, Diane's behavior today made her a suspect.

"Now what?" Aunt Thelma asked.

"I just think Diane's behavior today was suspicious. Regardless if everyone knew she was married to Lyle, her lack of emotion says something. And," I continued, following that thought thread, "there's a chance Lyle was poisoned, and Diane's bakery supplied the dessert table, didn't it?"

"My word. You think Diane killed Lyle?"

"Well, we know you didn't, unless you've got something else to say."

"It's just, I've known Diane for years! I can't imagine her hurting anyone."

"I don't know. Diane seems sort of like the quiet, mysterious type. She could've bewitched him, and it backfired."

Aunt Thelma looked alarmed.

"I'm sorry, I didn't mean to upset you. I'm just trying to help Vance come up with a defense for you, in case ..." I couldn't finish my sentence. It was too awful.

"In case I'm charged with Lyle's murder."

"Right."

Aunt Thelma and I were both silent as the gravity of the situation settled into the room. The feeling only lasted a minute until Aunt Thelma got a twinkle in her eye once more and said, "So you're working with Vance, huh?"

I tilted my head back and groaned. "You're impossible!"

"What? Vance is a nice man. You two used to love one another. Deeply. Why not give it another go?"

"I am not having this conversation right now." Or ever.

"What are you so afraid of?"

"I'm not afraid of anything. Will you knock it off? Now, I have a ton of work to do here, so if you don't mind."

"You're so testy," Aunt Thelma teased. "But I'll leave you alone, for now."

As she walked out the door, I closed my eyes and sighed, mentally calculating how many hours until I'd be back in Chicago.

I GOT UP EARLY the next morning and slipped my wand in my shorts pocket, pulling my polo shirt down over the top of it, and set out for Diane's bakery. The incident on the trail yesterday was still fresh in my mind, which is why I drove my rental car the short distance to the shops. I had slept rotten the night before, tossing and turning, fighting unknown assailants. I knew I wouldn't rest easy until the mystery of Lyle's death was solved. Which meant I needed to talk with Diane. I wanted to get a better read on the woman.

Bustling about in the sunlight-filled bakery, with a coffee pot in hand, Diane seemed like a completely different person. "Rough night?" she asked when I walked inside.

"Is it that obvious?" I said with a smile.

"How's Thelma holding up?"

"Better than me, I can tell you that."

"But you're worried about her."

I nodded.

Diane poured a cup of coffee and set it down in front of me along with a pastry on a plate. "Lemon scone, on the house. Cream and sugar are right behind you." I looked over my shoulder at the coffee station.

"Thanks so much." I went over and doctored up my coffee. A couple of older gentlemen sat at a table against the window, shooting the breeze like I'm sure they did every morning.

I took my coffee and scone over to one of the tables up front by the display case, where Diane was filling it with an assortment of tarts—peach, raspberry, and blackberry.

"You knew Lyle well, right?" I took a sip of my coffee.

Diane replied with a soft laugh. "You heard we were married."

"But you had been separated for a long while."

"That's true."

"And you never divorced?"

"Honestly, we just never got around to it. Our relationship was water under the bridge." Diane used her hand in a waving motion, like how a river would flow. "We were young, kids really. Over time we both grew in so many ways. Lyle was a good man, just not the right one for me. He felt the same way. I didn't harbor any ill will or bad feelings. It just is what it is, and we both moved on with our lives."

"What do you think happened yesterday?"

"Honestly, I'm not sure. I don't want to talk bad about your aunt, but it could be her fault. An accident of course," Diane quickly clarified.

A lump formed in my throat, and I swallowed it down. I'd thought the same thing. "I really hope someone else is to blame."

"Oh, me too, but I think you should prepare for the possibility." Diane gave me a sad smile. "Here, take these with you." She handed me a white pastry box full of tarts. "They won't take away your problems, but it'll give you something sweet to share with Thelma."

"Thanks, I appreciate it." I took the box from Diane. "Catch up with you later?"

"Absolutely. Our list of vendors is growing by the hour. I'll share it with you guys at the next meeting."

"Sounds good. Thanks again."

I felt guilty for my next stop, but I couldn't help it. I wanted to get a feel for Diane and Lyle's son on my own, and I wanted to be prepared with a list of suspects for Vance if it came down to it. I left my car parked where it was and wound my way down the shopping district's curved streets.

Everything about Village Square felt magical. You could feel it buzzing in the air—the enchanted energy. I wondered if it had always felt that way, and I had just gotten used to it. I walked past Clemmie's tea shop and waved through the front glass. She was with a customer looking at an antique tea set but glanced up and waved back. I would've stopped if I had the time, but I was on a mission. I looked for the spot where the wand shop used to be and did a double-take. Out was the dated storefront with its plastered wizard out front. In was a slick and modern wand boutique. Even the name had been given a facelift. Wally's Wands was now called Sticks. An improvement all around.

I looked in through the window at the updated space, which instantly gave off an urban vibe. It reminded me of a cell phone store or a name brand, high-end computer store. A large flat-screen television played a demo against the wall. A beautiful woman with windblown brown hair brandished a wand. She waved it majestically in the air. A gold stag shot out from it, running fiercely across the screen. There was no wand choosing the wizard here. The next scene showed two handsome men wearing sunglasses, sporting five o'clock shadows, dueling it out in the desert. Their movements were fast and fluid as spells shot out and were equally deflected. The tagline of the ad was, "Meet the new magic. Sticks 2.0."

"Well, this is fancy," I said when I entered. Displays promised wands that were intuitive, customizable, and one of a kind.

A man about my age walked around the counter to greet me. He was wearing black dress pants and a gray dress shirt. His hair was dark and curly. His smile, charming.

"Welcome to Sticks. How can I help you?" he asked.

"I had no idea wands were so high tech," I remarked.

"Welcome to the future."

"I guess so." I looked around at the touchscreen displays and sample wands sitting behind glass cases. "I've been out of the loop for a while. Are all wand-makers like this now?"

"Not yet, but they will be. I'm Peter."

"Angelica," I said, shaking his hand.

"Are you in the market for a new wand?" Peter asked.

"So I'm told."

Peter looked at me, waiting for me to elaborate.

"I've been in Chicago for the last decade and then some. My aunt kept my childhood wand for me. I think it's from the nineties."

"An antique," Peter remarked with a smile. I found myself smiling in return. Then Peter put two and two together. "You're Angelica Nightingale. Thelma's niece."

"I am. I'm so sorry for your loss."

Peter nodded. I wasn't sure how he was going to react next. Did he think my aunt killed his dad? If so, would he lash out at me for coming into his store?

But Peter didn't. Instead he said, "How about we get started then?" as he led me over to one of the touch displays.

"What is this?"

"This is where the magic happens. You input all of your specs, what you intend to use your wand primarily for, say charms or defense work. Add in your dimensions like height and arm length, and the program creates your perfect wand."

"Really? That's crazy." I went through some of the touchscreens, noting transfiguration as one of the options. I selected it. Peter raised his eyebrows, seeming surprised by my choice. I didn't elaborate. If I was going to replace my wand, I wanted to make sure it could do everything that I was technically capable of. After a few more selections, an hourglass on the screen appeared, and within seconds I had a result: a nine-inch fir wand with a dual-core—unicorn hair for charm work and dragon heartstring for transfiguration. The grip was customizable with pearlized inlays and gem accents, reminding me of the mother of pearl accent on Aunt Thelma's wand. The wands were almost like jewelry. I guess the saying is true that the apple doesn't fall far from the tree.

Peter took a similar-sized wand out from the display case and handed it to me.

I hesitated.

"Don't worry, the core's empty," he assured me.

"Thanks. It's been years since I've practiced. I just don't want to hurt anyone." Myself included. I had to admit the wand felt nice in my hand, and as a bonus, it was smaller than the one that I was currently carrying.

"All wands come with a lifetime guarantee that the core will remain charged, and a ninety-day, no questions asked return policy," Peter said.

Did I want a new wand? Was I ever going to use it? I didn't know the answer to either one of those questions. I was betting the wand wasn't cheap, either.

"Can I see the one you're carrying now?" Peter asked.

Reluctantly, I took out my wand and handed it over, trying not to look embarrassed. The dated piece didn't match me or my professional personality.

Peter took the wand from my hand and walked over to the power reader, clicking the wood between two sensors. The digital display on the bottom blinked red like a dead battery would. As if proving a point, Peter took his own wand out and switched it with mine. The digital readout went from red to yellow to green, maxing out the power display. "Hate to break it to you, but your core is dead."

I let out a breath. A broken wand wouldn't do me any good. "How much is the new one?"

While Peter rang me up with a promise my wand would be ready in a day, as all the components were in stock and he'd personally assemble it, I took a stab and asked what would happen to the jewelry store.

"I don't know, liquidate the inventory? I'm not sure. We weren't close."

"Oh, sorry. I shouldn't have assumed."

"It's alright." But I could tell from the look in Peter's eyes that it wasn't. I didn't know what to make of that.

CHAPTER NINE

On the drive back to the inn, I thought about Peter and Diane. They were complex individuals with more to them than met the eye. I was just about to cross over the creek when I saw Aunt Thelma walking over the footbridge. She was dressed head to toe in white, even donning a formal hat, her strawberry blonde hair hidden beneath its brim.

I slowed and rolled down the window. "Where are you off to?"

"Me? I could say the same thing to you. You took off this morning before I could even catch you."

"Stopped by the bakery." I held up the pastry box for evidence. "And bought a new wand."

Aunt Thelma walked over to the window. "Good. Now give me a ride." She opened the door and climbed in.

"Where are we going?"

"Silverlake Legal. They've summoned me to the reading of Lyle's will. It would be nice if you came."

I glanced at my aunt before making a right-hand turn and driving past the inn. The law office was in the residential area on the other side of the lake, not too far up the road from the post office.

"Lyle left you something?"

"It would appear so." Aunt Thelma looked out the window, and I could tell she didn't want to talk about it.

"That explains why Boyd couldn't take your case."

"What in the world are you talking about?"

"I called his office first before hiring Vance, but he said that it was a conflict of interest."

"I suppose that does make sense."

It took less than ten minutes to make it around the lake by car. In no time, we were parking in the back lot of the attorney's office. The single-story, white-washed brick building had a postage-stamp-sized front yard that butted up to the sidewalk. The only greenery came from the two potted arborvitaes, shaped like corkscrews, that flanked the entrance.

I opened the heavy front door for Aunt Thelma and walked in after her.

"Thelma! Boyd was relieved to hear you'd be able to make it on such short notice," Cindy said. "And you must be Angelica," she added. Cindy was new since I'd worked there.

I waved hello. The door opened once more behind me, and I stepped aside to make room for Peter to walk in. Our eyes met, and he looked away. Clearly, he wasn't expecting me to be there.

"Mr. Andrews is expecting you in the conference room. Let me lead you back."

Cindy came around the counter and opened a side door, much like you'd find at a doctor's office. The back of the house held a couple of different offices. Floor-to-ceiling glass windows made them look larger than they were. Vertical blinds hung from the windows, offering a bit of privacy.

"Right in here." Cindy held her arm out for us to walk in. A sizeable, oval-shaped ,oak table stood in the middle of the room. A beverage table was set up in the back with coffee service and a pitcher filled with iced water and lemon slices. Boyd and Diane were already waiting.

"Can I get you anything to drink?" Cindy asked, touching my forearm.

"No, I'm fine. Thank you."

"Angelica, good to see you," Boyd said. He was a plump, older man who favored suspenders and bow ties —an affection that seemed to only grow with age given the coordinating striped set he wore now.

"Likewise," I replied.

"Although, I wish it were under happier circumstances." Boyd rocked back on his heels. A dangerous move, seeing as he could topple right on over.

"Me too," I said.

"Seems we're all here. Let's get to it. Shall we?"

Boyd sat down and opened the leather portfolio before him. "This right here is the last will and testament of Lyle Peters. You're all here today because he mentioned you specifically in his final wishes." Boyd stopped himself there. "Well, not you, Angelica."

I held up my hand. "Don't worry, I know."

Boyd continued. "'To my son, Peter.'" Peter's ears perked up. "'I want you to know that money won't buy happiness. To find it, you must look within.'"

Boyd retrieved an antique-looking key from his shirt pocket and passed it across the table to Peter. Peter picked it up and examined it, looking rather unimpressed. He put it back down on the table and folded his arms across his chest.

"'To Diane, I leave you Mr. Fitzgerald. I know you will take great care of him.'"

Diane nodded as if she wasn't surprised. "Elizabeth will be thrilled," Diane remarked. "He's her brother," she added.

"Huh?" I replied.

"They're cats," Aunt Thelma whispered.

"Oh, got it."

"'To Thelma Nightingale, the true love of my life, I leave you with my home and all of my financial assets.'" Boyd looked at Thelma over the rim of his wire glasses. "'This includes the jewelry store, inventory, and his 401k.'"

"Wait, what? You and Lyle?" The question was out of my mouth before I could stop myself.

Before my aunt could reply, Peter threw himself back from the table. "This is ridiculous."

"Peter," Diane tried to stop her son from losing his cool, but it was too late.

"Would it have killed him to give me a dime? His own son!" Peter beat his fist on the table. "I thought maybe he'd surprise me. Guess the joke's on me." Peter looked up at the ceiling. "Idiot." His face flushed with anger. "I'm out of here." Peter made eye contact with his mother and then stormed out, leaving Diane to scramble after him.

"Did you know?" I whispered to my aunt.

"That Lyle would leave me everything? No. I expected a locket or something sentimental, not this."

I then remembered Lyle's complaints about business being slow and needing money at the bank and wondered just how much Aunt Thelma had inherited. Was it really worth Peter getting that upset over?

"Can I ask how much?" I asked Boyd.

"If it's alright with Thelma."

She nodded that it was.

"Liquid assets and the house?" Boyd whistled. "Over a million."

"A million?" That didn't make any sense. I wanted to say as much, but for once, I kept my mouth shut.

Aunt Thelma dabbed at the corner of her eyes. "Oh, Lyle." The words were whisper soft.

Oh, Lyle was right.

"Mind if I take this?" I asked Boyd, referencing the

key. "I'm going to see Peter in the next day or so. I can try and give it to him again."

"Be my guest. I don't think he'll be back here anytime soon," Boyd replied.

"Thanks. Are we good to go?"

Boyd nodded. "I'll be in touch, Thelma."

We said our goodbyes and walked back to the car.

"You have some explaining to do." I buckled myself in the car.

"What term did you use?"

"When?"

"When you got here. You said your relationship was very new."

"Obviously, yours wasn't if the man left you a million dollars!"

"Let's just say the man had been sweet on me for years, and I finally gave in."

"And Diane knew?"

"Of course. She's one of my closest friends. Besides, her relationship with Lyle was long over before he pursued me. I can promise you that."

We were stopped at the town's one stoplight while I waited to turn left.

After a minute, I couldn't help but ask, "What's up with Lyle and Peter's relationship?"

"I don't know. I stayed away from that." Aunt Thelma held up her hands in a stopping motion. "But, I do know that Peter's very driven, which makes Lyle's final message to him all the more fitting."

"You don't think money can buy happiness?"

"Why, you do?" Aunt Thelma leaned over in her seat and looked at me.

"I'm just saying it can't hurt." I also couldn't help but think that Peter and I were more alike than different.

"How's the festival planning coming?" Aunt Thelma asked, changing the subject.

"Good, I guess. There's still a ton to do." I thought for a moment. "Do you still have the old mailing lists I created?"

"Oh, I don't know. They're probably still in the same drawer."

"Let's see if we can find it and get a mailer out. Offer up a discount to guests for repeat stays," I suggested.

"That's a good idea."

"What about email addresses? Have you been collecting them?"

"What in the world would I do that for?"

"So you can market to your customers. You know, marketing, advertising, tactics you use to bring in business?"

"People just usually show up."

"Except when they don't."

We pulled into the inn's parking lot. "I'm going to go upstairs and write some more content for the website and then create an online sign-up sheet for volunteers to help with setting up for the dance." I also needed to

see if any high schoolers might want to help with the
face painting and if Mr. McCormick would donate
pumpkins for the carving contest. My mental to-do list
was getting longer by the second.

"While you do that, I'll go upstairs and change, and
maybe we can meet for lunch on the patio in an hour,"
Aunt Thelma suggested.

"Sounds good." I walked through the lobby and was
headed straight upstairs when I stopped dead in my
tracks.

"Allen." I smacked my palm on my forehead as I
stared at the man I was dating, standing next to the
registration desk. He looked somewhat out of place
with his ironed khakis and calculator tucked under his
arm, staring at the tourist brochures. There was something else, too. He was glowing. Not his complexion,
but rather his whole body had a halo-like glow
around it.

"What? What's wrong?" Allen said, looking behind
his shoulder.

"Nothing," I said, shaking my head. I couldn't
explain to him why he looked the way he did to me or
the fact that I had completely forgotten that he was
coming.

"You must be Angelica's special friend," Aunt
Thelma said with a smile. "Come, come. Let me show
you the back office where you can work your magic."
She emphasized the last word.

I gave my aunt a look that suggested she knock it

off. She replied with a cheery smile as she looped her arm through Allen's and steered him to the office. Allen looked behind him to make sure I was coming along. I shuffled after them.

"Percy picked up the computer for you and whatever's in that box over there." Aunt Thelma pointed to a large brown box that said some assembly required in thick black letters.

"That would be the office chair," I supplied.

"Well then, I guess you two have plenty to do. I'll leave you alone to get to it." Aunt Thelma winked and walked away. Allen looked around at the cramped quarters and the stacked ledgers, clearly not impressed. If he thought this looked bad, he should've seen it before I spent hours straightening it up.

"Was your trip okay?" I asked, trying to break the awkwardness hanging in the air.

"It was the strangest thing."

"Strange how?"

"I don't remember much after talking to your aunt on the phone." Allen looked off in the distance as if trying to make sense of it all. "One minute, I was in Chicago, and the next, here. I'm not sure what happened."

"You don't say."

"I don't even know if I called into work."

"Really, huh?"

"But I have my calculator." Allen held it up as proof. "So I must've gone to the office."

"Jet lag, maybe?" I offered up, even though I knew exactly what happened. The question was why my aunt felt the need to bewitch Allen into coming here. I was going to have a talk with her sooner rather than later.

"And my cell phone won't work." Allen held up his phone for emphasis. "Won't hold a charge."

"Maybe try my charger?" I pointed to the one I left on the desk from the day before.

Allen picked it up and examined it as if to see if it was up to par. "I have a spare in my bag." He set my charger back down. I shouldn't be surprised that he preferred his charger to mine, but it still irked me. They were the exact same kind.

"Would you like something to drink?" I offered after he plugged in his phone.

"Sure. Bottled water, sparkling," Allen spoke as if I were a waitress.

"How does bottled water, plain sound?"

"Perhaps I should just get to work then." Allen eyed the dated computer chair before looking at the box.

"I'll start on the chair," I offered.

Allen nodded and reluctantly pulled the old chair out, tried to push the exposed foam back into the rip, gave up, and finally sat down.

I opened my laptop in front of him and quickly explained what I had been up to—inputting the hotel's expenses into new software that I would then transfer to the new computer. "But everything was done on paper," I explained, referencing the binders behind me.

"Everything?" Allen looked at me in disbelief.

"Everything, and we have to balance the books. I need to find out who is owed money and how much and compare it to what we have in the bank." Hopefully, the inn wasn't in the red.

I plopped a stack of bills in front of Allen.

"All these are unpaid?"

"I have no idea. That's what we have to find out."

Allen didn't look amused, but nevertheless, he got to work sorting through the debts and inputting them into the computer while I tackled the new chair.

CHAPTER TEN

Thirty silent minutes later, I was no closer to assembling the chair, and my frustrations were ratcheting up by the second. I had all the screws laid out along with the allen wrench (the irony was not lost on me), but I couldn't figure out what piece was Part A so I could screw into Part B, and I was pretty sure I was missing Part C. I looked over at Allen. He was busy inputting numbers and cross-referencing dated spreadsheets, entirely in his element.

"You know, on second thought, maybe we do have sparkling water." I stood up, abandoning my project. If we didn't, I could see about conjuring a bottle up from in town. "Let me go check." I retreated from the office before Allen could respond. Not that he would when he was absorbed in his work. Believe me, I'd already tried. My inquiries into his past vacations were met with stony silence. Charming.

The moment I stepped out of the office, I shook off the awkwardness that clung to my skin like a wet dog.

Percy looked over his shoulder with a sheepish expression.

"What are you doing?"

"Nothing."

I looked at the counter. A small pile of wadded-up paper the size of peas and a straw sat beside him. The first round of spitballs stuck to the wallpaper behind him. "Wanna give it a try?" Percy motioned with his head down to the straw. "You can pretend it's his face." By he, Percy meant Allen.

I smirked. "Maybe later. Do you know where my aunt is?"

"Lunch, outside."

"Thanks."

I walked through the lobby and directly out onto the back deck. The sun was shining brightly. A cool breeze blew in across the lake. And if I closed my eyes and took a deep breath, I'd feel loads better. But I didn't do that. Instead, I let my frustrations out on my aunt.

"You bewitched him to come here, didn't you." The words flew out of my mouth as I approached her. Aunt Thelma sat with a cobb salad before her and a glass of white wine.

"Is there a problem?"

"Yes, there's a problem. Why would you do that?"

"I wanted you to see that Allen wasn't right for you."

"How can you say that? You don't even know him."

"No, but I know you—the real you. You don't belong with a stick."

"Allen is not a stick-in-the-mud."

Aunt Thelma looked at me knowingly over the rim of her glass.

"He is too, and you know it, which is exactly why you're with him. He's safe."

I opened my mouth to retort but couldn't think of a thing to say.

"Quit running away and hiding from every feeling you have. Emotions are meant to be felt."

"Easy for you to say," I blurted out.

"Easy for me to say? I finally open my heart to someone, and he drops dead right in front of me. People think I killed him. Me!"

My anger deflated like a popped balloon. "I'm sorry. Forget I said anything."

My aunt's eyes softened. "All I want is for you to open your eyes and be honest with yourself. Does Allen make you happy?"

"What do you mean by happy? What does that have to do with anything?" I scoffed.

"Were you excited to see him just now? Did your pulse race? Did butterflies flutter in your tummy?"

"My stomach is just fine."

Aunt Thelma looked at me and sighed. "You know what I mean."

I exhaled. Yes, I did know what she meant.

"You didn't even remember he was coming."

"Hey, I've been a bit preoccupied with everything," I countered before shaking my head. "Listen, Allen is a decent guy. He has a good job. A nice condo. He dresses well."

"You're not buying a new car. You're looking for someone to love."

"I don't know about that." Love wasn't for me. I tried that once. It didn't work out. I wasn't going to make the same mistake again.

"Well then, that's a shame."

I hated the way my aunt looked at me, but I didn't know what to say. Instead, I changed the subject. "I meant to ask, why is Allen glowing?"

"You don't remember?"

"Remember what?"

"Mortals glow here. It's how us witches know not to perform any magic in front of him."

"Huh, I don't think I ever knew that."

"Well, now you do. Mortals don't come here very often, but when they do, we have to be able to spot them."

"Got it." I then remembered Allen's request. "Can you get some sparkling bottled water?" I waved my hand in the air, suggesting she use magic.

"Check the wine cooler. Behind the champagne. I believe there's a bottle."

"Oh. Who knew?"

"We're just full of surprises here."

"Speaking of which, did you ever find your wand?"

"Afraid not. But Peter offered to make me a new one with a location charm. Isn't that wonderful?"

"It is, and smart. Guess I better get back to it."

"Enjoy," Aunt Thelma replied with a knowing smile. I tried not to scowl.

As MUCH AS I didn't want to, I thought about my conversation with my aunt the rest of the afternoon while Allen and I worked.

"What do you say we go out for dinner? I know it's not Paulina's, but there's a nice restaurant one town over. I think you'd like it," I said after assembling the chair and setting up the new computer. I even installed the accounting software and researched online reservation systems a bit more. The inn didn't need all the bells and whistles we offered in Chicago, but they needed something more than the pen-and-paper system they used out front. For now, I requested the Mystic Inn be added to the online Witches Network travel guide and paid for an advertising spot on the network (out of my own money because who knew if Aunt Thelma had it). It wasn't much, but it was a start. We had to get the word out about the festival now.

Allen glanced up from the ledgers, a pencil poised in hand. He looked skeptical. "Dinner?"

"You do have to eat."

Allen's eyes wandered over to his briefcase. I'd bet a witch's hat it was stocked with his favorite granola bars and maybe a box of high-fiber cereal.

"Doesn't an evening out sound nice?" I asked in all seriousness.

"I suppose. Can we make it an early dinner? I find that if I eat too late, I have a hard time falling asleep."

"Yeah, that's fine with me. How about I go up and change right now, and we can leave in thirty minutes?"

"I guess that would be all right."

"Okay. I'll meet you in the lobby shortly."

The Grove was the type of restaurant that people dressed up for. Thankfully, I had packed a nice dress, seeing as I thought I'd be attending a funeral. I shook my head as I thought about how different the last forty-eight hours had gone compared to what I had expected. As for Allen, well, he always wore button-up shirts and sweater vests. It was just his style, even for a summer evening out. I, on the other hand, took it a step further —blow drying my hair straight, adding an extra coat of mascara, and slipping on a pair of high heels.

I went down to the lobby planning to wait for Allen, but he was already there.

"Are you ready to go?" he asked, glancing up from his phone, which was magically back to working.

"Yes, you?"

"Sure, I guess so."

"Don't sound so excited," I said playfully.

"I'm not," Allen replied flatly.

"Right, got it." I smoothed out my dress.

"You kids have fun," Percy said from behind the counter. I gave him a wave goodbye. He replied by sticking his tongue out behind Allen's back. I smirked.

"Strange man," Allen said as we walked out to my car, referring to the poltergeist.

"He can be." I opened my car door and thought if only Allen knew the half of it.

It took about a half-hour to get to The Grove, and I was surprised how easily I remembered how to get there.

The restaurant was located in downtown Jackson, further up the river. The same town the computer and office chair had come from. The downtown area was built up around the riverfront, with restaurants offering outdoor waterfront seating along with inside dining.

"Would you like to sit inside or out?" the hostess asked.

Allen and I both spoke at the same time.

"Inside," he said.

"Outside," I replied.

Allen was taken aback by my answer. "But the mosquitoes," he rationalized.

"They're not too bad tonight," I remarked. For the record, I hadn't seen any, but I couldn't promise that one wouldn't interrupt our meal. Allen looked disgusted at the thought of a bug landing on his dinner. "Inside would be fine," I replied to the hostess.

After accepting our menus and making our water

selection (sparkling bottled for Allen, of course), I ordered a glass of wine.

"Do you have Clos de los Siete? It's a bordeaux," Allen said while skimming the restaurant's expansive wine menu. The satiny black book offered at least fifty different wines.

"That doesn't sound familiar, but I can check with the sommelier. Is there another bordeaux you'd like if not?" the hostess offered.

"Can you just check with the sommelier? Thanks." Allen closed the wine menu and looked at me. I was staring at him like he had two heads. At least he wasn't glowing anymore.

"What?"

"That's the wine you drink at Paulina's," I said.

"So?"

"Don't you ever try anything new?"

"Not if I can help it." Allen picked up the dinner menu, and I had a sinking feeling this date wasn't going to get any better.

Shortly after, we were already eating the main course. Allen passed up on the appetizers and picked half of his salad out onto his bread plate, which also sat untouched. "It's not whole wheat," he said when the waitress served the breadbasket.

I glanced over at the couple sitting in the corner booth, side by side. It looked to be a romantic dinner. The man had his arm around the woman's neck. They were drinking red wine, looking into each other's eyes.

Jealousy uncoiled in my belly, followed by recognition when I caught the man's eye. It was Diane and Roger. Diane smiled. Roger nuzzled her neck. They looked happy.

Darn it. I thought of Aunt Thelma again.

"Something the matter? "Allen asked, following my gaze.

"No, it's just someone I know. I'm surprised to see them, that's all," which was the truth. I hadn't known they were together.

"They look like a nice couple."

"Mmm-hmm."

I would've walked over and said hi, but I didn't want to intrude on their romantic evening. At least someone was having one.

* * *

When we got back to the inn, it was just after seven o'clock.

"Do you want to have a glass of wine on the patio and watch the sunset?" I was still trying to salvage the evening, or perhaps our relationship. I wanted to feel something, make a spark fly between the two of us, but it wasn't happening. There wasn't even an ember smoldering below the surface.

"Didn't you already have a glass of wine with dinner?" Allen asked.

"It was just a suggestion," I replied, feeling judged.

"No, I'm going to take one of the binders and head up to my room and call it an early night."

"Okay, well, I hope you're able to get some rest."

"Me too. I should've brought my own pillows. I don't know what I was thinking."

Allen walked away. "Good night," I said, barely above a whisper. I sighed. All dressed up and no place to go, I thought, feeling disappointed that Allen hadn't even told me I looked nice.

Aunt Thelma was right. Why was I dating him? I shook my head. I didn't have the mental energy to dissect my relationship.

Maybe tomorrow.

Instead, I decided to keep with my suggested plan and watch the sunset on the patio. Heck, go big or go home, I thought, as I took a bottle of champagne out of the wine cooler. The sight of the last bottle of sparkling water behind it irked me more than it should have.

As I took the champagne out, I pondered when the last time was I drank a glass of bubbly just because— not toasting someone at a wedding or clinking glasses at a New Year's Eve party—just a glass of champagne while watching the sunset. It wasn't this year, or maybe even this decade. The realization was depressing. If I kept up with this train of thought, I was sure to be crying by nightfall.

To new beginnings, I thought to myself as I filled my champagne flute. The water across the lake was calm. Cicadas buzzed in the distance, and somewhere high in a tree, an owl awoke with a hoot. I breathed in the beauty of nature and sat on the patio steps where the stone steps met the beach. The sand was still warm on my toes. I took a sip of champagne and smiled. It felt good to be a rebel.

"What are we celebrating?" The voice came from behind me and made me jump.

"You scared me half to death," I said to Vance.

"Can I join you?" he asked.

"I don't have another glass."

"Ah, that's okay. I can drink out of the bottle."

"You would too, wouldn't you?"

"What can I say? I'm a simple guy."

I handed Vance my glass to hold as I ducked back inside and fetched one for him.

"So, what are we celebrating?" Vance asked again.

"Who says we have to be celebrating something?"

"I don't know, champagne, sunset, you in a beautiful dress. You look great, by the way."

I looked down. "Thanks." I clinked my glass with Vance's.

I went back to answering Vance's question. "Honestly, I thought, what the heck. You only live once, right? Why save the good stuff for special occasions."

"I can drink to that." Vance clinked his glass with mine once more, and we both took another sip.

"What are you doing here?" I asked.

"I came over to run some things by your aunt."

"You heard about the inheritance."

"I did." Vance held the champagne glass with both hands between his knees.

"Did you know they were a couple?"

"Did you?" Vance countered.

"Not a clue, but then again, I hadn't spoken to Aunt Thelma in a while."

Vance cocked his head. "You hadn't? Why not?" He took another sip of his drink, and I topped both of our glasses off before answering.

"I guess I got too busy. Too caught up in work. I forgot to spend time with anyone that mattered."

Vance nodded. "Been there, done that. That's why I moved back."

"I don't think that's an option for me."

"Why not? You only live once, remember?" Vance downed the rest of his champagne and handed the glass to me. "I've got to run. Thanks for the drink."

"Sure." Vance was halfway up the stairs before I asked, "How bad is it?"

"Your aunt?"

I nodded.

"It doesn't look good, but we'll figure it out."

"I hope so."

"Good night, Angie."

"Good night." I turned to look back at the sunset and found myself wondering how in the world I was ever going to sleep that night.

CHAPTER ELEVEN

—————

It turns out, when you drink half a bottle of champagne, you sleep like a baby.

But the headache in the morning is killer.

I opened my eyes. The lavender-painted walls swam into focus. I was going to have to learn how to seize the day with a little less alcohol.

I laid in bed extra long, scrolling through my phone. I wasn't in any hurry to go downstairs and work one-on-one with Allen in the office, which is why when Peter's text came through that my wand was ready for pick up, I jumped at the chance to head out.

Maybe not quite so much jumped, but rather slowly got out of bed, took two Tylenol, showered, and then left.

It was much quieter this morning by the shops, seeing it was Sunday morning, and most places didn't open until after noon. Sticks was one of the exceptions.

I opened the door and walked inside. Everything looked the same as the day before, including Peter. He came out from the back, wearing the same black pants and gray shirt from yesterday. He rubbed his eyes and yawned.

"You got here fast," he remarked.

"I was looking for a reason to escape for a bit."

"Been there." We were quiet for a moment. "Sorry about yesterday. At the attorney's office?" Peter elaborated in case there was any confusion.

"No, I understand." At least I thought I did.

"I wasn't expecting your aunt to inherit everything."

"She wasn't either. I didn't even know they were dating."

"I knew that, but I didn't think he'd cut me out."

"Any idea why?" I wasn't sure if I was prying too much.

"As I said, we weren't close, but we were working on it. I'd talked to him the last couple of months about investing in the business. All this stuff," Peter used his hands to show the expansion of the room, "costs money. Capital. I thought he was starting to listen to me, to see the potential. He knew I needed the money, but instead of helping me, now I'm stuck with a business partner—something I didn't want to do.

"You are? Who?"

"Charles Barker."

"The bank manager?"

"That's the one. He's great with investments, which

is why he has the cash for a business, but it wasn't what I was looking for.

"That stinks, but at least you have financing now."

"I suppose. I honestly just wanted a loan, but the next thing I knew, he sent over a business agreement."

"Did you sign it?"

"Not yet, but I'm going to have to if I want Sticks to hit the global market." Peter rubbed his weary eyes with the palms of his hands.

"You know, just because your dad didn't leave you any money doesn't mean he didn't believe in you."

"Really, because that's exactly what it feels like. All that garbage about money not buying happiness is a slap in the face."

"That reminds me. You left the key in the conference room." I took it out of my pocket.

"Keep it. I don't ever want to see it again."

"Oh-kay." I repocketed the key. We were silent again. "If it makes you feel any better, when my mom died, there wasn't any money to leave. It was up to my aunt to provide for me."

"And your dad?"

"Good question." I left my remark at that. Truth be told, my dad abandoned us long before my mom's accident. The first time I gave myself a tail, he hightailed it out of our lives. Turned out, Mom hadn't told him she was a witch. They clearly never visited Silverlake.

"Have you been here all night?" I asked, changing the subject.

"I couldn't sleep, so I figured I might as well work. It usually helps me clear my head."

"And did it?"

Peter chuckled. "No, not really. But I did get your wand done. Want to see it?"

"Absolutely."

Peter disappeared in the back for a moment and came back carrying a sleek white box. He handed it over. I walked over to the glass display case and pulled the box apart. Sitting on a cushion of black velvet was my wand. I hesitated, only for a second, before picking up the smooth, rounded handle with blue opal inlay. The added touch was beautiful and unexpected. I held still for a moment and felt the magic tingle through me, awakening something deep inside. I couldn't explain it, but for the first time, in a very long time, I felt like a witch. It was unnerving.

"Whoa." I sat the wand back down and shook out my hand.

"Is it too much?" Peter's face was etched with concern.

"No. I don't think so. It's just me. It's been a while." I took a deep breath and exhaled, picking the wand back up. The same intense rush of power moved through me, only this time, it made me smile. I looked about the shop to find something to test it out on, coming to land on a paper clip next to the cash register.

"Do you mind?"

"No, by all means." Peter extended his hand. I

pointed the tip of the wand at the paper clip and muttered a quick incantation, believing the words to be true. That was the key to making magic work— believing it was possible. A blue light shot from the wand and landed on the paper clip, instantly transforming it into a butterfly. The creature was beautiful, with large patches of metallic blue, teal, and purple painted on its wings. It was a combination of all my favorite colors. The butterfly took off and fluttered about the store. Peter walked over, opened the door, and the butterfly followed him, flying out into the morning light.

Peter looked back at me, and we both smiled.

"I haven't done that spell in years," I confessed.

"Well, you'd never know it. You're a gifted witch, Angelica."

"I guess I am." How had I forgotten so much?

I went back to the Mystic Inn, feeling more like myself than I had in years. It was an odd feeling, and one that my former self wanted to bottle back up, but I knew I couldn't. I couldn't go back to being the woman I was before, the one that I had convinced myself I wanted to be—that I had to be—when clearly it didn't make me happy. Performing that spell was the first time that I had truly felt alive in a long time. I sat with that thought as I entered the inn's lobby.

Allen was behind the reception counter, going over numbers with my aunt. She smiled when she saw me, and I returned the expression. Allen briefly glanced up before returning his pencil to paper.

"Good morning?" Aunt Thelma asked me.

"It was. Very eye-opening," I confessed.

"Thelma Nightingale?" Amber's voice came from behind me. I hadn't even seen the deputy in the parking lot. "You're officially under arrest for the murder of Lyle Peters. You need to come with me." Amber had her handcuffs at the ready.

"No, you can't!" I couldn't believe it. Amber couldn't arrest Aunt Thelma. I still hadn't figured out what really happened.

"What is going on here?" Allen looked up, rather annoyed at being interrupted. He quickly took in the scene. His face paled.

Without even thinking, I pulled out my brand-new wand and pointed it at him. "Glacio," I commanded, and Allen froze.

"Nice," Aunt Thelma remarked.

"Sorry, I panicked," I replied.

"Don't look at me. Mortals are outside my jurisdiction. But you do need to come with me," Amber said to Thelma.

"Just let me grab my purse," Thelma replied.

"I'll call Vance," I added. "Percy?" I hollered out into the lobby. The poltergeist readily appeared. "Can you help me move Allen to the office?"

Percy took in Allen's frozen state and let out a

hearty laugh. "What took you so long? Talk about a square."

"Just help me, will you?" I knew Allen would be safe in the back, and no one would bother him. I also knew sooner rather than later, I would have to unfreeze him and alter his memory just a tad. None of which I was looking forward to.

I dialed Vance's number while Amber read Aunt Thelma her rights. "Vance, it's Angie. Amber's just arrested Aunt Thelma."

"I'm not surprised. The coroner just released the cause of death. A curse killed Lyle."

"How can they be certain?"

"His blood turned black."

"Oh, gross."

"You asked."

That I did. "I guess that means he wasn't poisoned."

"You thought he was poisoned?"

"It was just an idea seeing desserts were at the meeting."

"From who?"

"Diane. Her bakery catered it."

"Well, she might have a motive."

"Yeah, I thought that too, but not so much after I talked to her. Plus, I saw her last night on a date at The Grove."

"Oh, so that's why you were dressed up last night. Lucky guy."

I didn't reply to Vance's comment. "My point is, I think Diane has moved on with her life."

"She's still on my list of suspects," Vance remarked. "I'm going to head down to the station and see what else I can find out."

"Do you know if they ever found Lyle's wand?"

"Not that I've heard. But I'll ask."

I hung up with Vance and thought that while he did that, I would head down to the bookstore and see if Misty knew anything.

———

WHEN I GOT to the bookstore, I was shocked to see it was packed. A line snaked around the checkout counter, and Misty was moving a mile a minute.

"What's going on?" I asked.

"I was worried about business being slow, so I offered up a brown bag special. Fill a bag with books and pay ten bucks. I had no idea how successful it would be." Misty ripped off a receipt and handed it to the customer in front of her. "Thanks so much," she said to them.

I leaned forward. "Do you know if they found Lyle's wand?"

"No, they didn't. I'm supposed to keep an eye out for it."

"Do you mind if I look upstairs?"

"No, help yourself. Everything is open to the

public." I had a feeling that finding Lyle's wand and maybe even my aunt's would be the key to solving the case.

"Let me see if I can get a worker to help me out up here. I need to talk to you about something else." Misty looked serious.

"Okay, I'll be upstairs searching."

It was a task easier said than done as the second story was just as busy as the first. I had to keep saying, "excuse me," as I looked under the bookshelves, even going so far as to pick up every book on the shelf to look underneath them and open random ones to search within. I examined the chair cushions in various seating areas and under the upstairs rug, but no wand.

Misty met me a few minutes later. "Any luck?"

"Not yet." I was standing on a chair, looking at the top of one of the shelves. "What's up?" I dusted my hands and stepped down.

"I think someone tried to break in here last night."

"Are you serious? How?"

"The back door right off the patio. There were marks, like a crowbar or something."

"Did you call the police?"

"I didn't. I figured the person didn't get in, and they got what they deserved."

"How so?"

"The wards. If anyone tries to break in, they'll be nursing some pretty nasty blisters come morning."

"I bet whoever tried to break in was looking for the wand, and maybe they're the real killer."

"You think so?"

"I do. Which means it's here somewhere."

"But where? I feel like the deputies have searched everywhere."

"Should we try a summoning charm?"

"She already tried it. It didn't work."

"Who?"

"Amber."

"What the heck? Why wouldn't it work?" Summoning charms were pretty straightforward. They weren't complex like tracing spells, which combined magic and emotions. Those spells were often used in missing persons cases and required you to love the person. Summoning only required you to picture the item.

"I have no idea. Magic theory was never my strong suit. Listen, I have to get back downstairs. You're welcome to keep on looking anywhere you think it might be."

CHAPTER TWELVE

I still hadn't found it an hour later, and I wasn't sure where else to look. I was going to have to change tactics. If I couldn't find the wand, maybe I could discover what secrets Lyle might have been hiding. Someone killed him for a reason. I had to find out why.

In a flash, I had a brilliant idea. Either that or it was incredibly stupid. Only time would tell. I said goodbye to Misty and set my plan into motion. As I walked along the curved path, I tried to think of another solution but came up empty.

No, this was the best way.

I couldn't wait until nightfall. The jewelry store probably had wards on it like the bookstore, even if I could break-in.

I dipped into the alleyway between the bookstore and the cafe. Thankfully it was deserted as I'd hoped. "Please work." My voice trembled from nerves. I looked both ways to make sure I truly was alone. Convinced it was now or never, I gripped the tiger's eye stone around my neck, closed my eyes, and said the incantation that would transform me into my feline alter ego: "Metamorfóno alithís ousía." The necklace channeled the magic and released it in a burst. Bright, white light surrounded me. Heat flooded my body as atoms rearranged themselves and altered my reality. In an instant, the spell was complete. My heart stayed the same, but everything else changed. I looked down at the ground, which was suddenly very close, and held my paws out in front of me before testing them out like a cat does when they step in water, shaking each one out.

Pride built in my chest, and it came out as a purr. I trotted toward the jewelry store, head held high like I was the king of the jungle. One thing I had going for me was that very few people would recognize me in this form. Aunt Thelma, Vance, and Clemmie were the only three people I could think of, and two of them were occupied.

Not many witches could transform. It was a trait passed down from one's mother to the oldest child. My mother had been able to do it. I remembered the cat she would morph into, a beautiful white Himalayan with thick white fur and sparkling green eyes. They were the same color my eyes were now. I couldn't think about that now, though. I had a jewelry store to sneak into.

I was sitting in front of the shop, partially hidden

by a planter box and debating which entrance to stake out when someone picked me up from behind.

I panicked as my feet left the ground, scurrying to get away, but the child held on tight.

"ROWW!" I cried.

"Look, Mama, a kitty." The girl held me at arm's length. "And she doesn't have a collar." The girl hugged me tightly to her chest. I used my paws to try to push off and lean away. But the more I squirmed, the harder the kid held on.

"Oh, honey, let her go. I'm sure she belongs to someone here," the mother replied.

"But Mama, there's a lot of cars around here. What if somebody hits her?" The young girl's bottom lip quivered.

The mom seemed to hesitate, realizing that her daughter was right. If I didn't think fast, I'd be headed to animal control or, worse, the vet. I didn't want to claw or scratch the child, who had me in a fierce embrace, but I couldn't squirm away.

I let out a pitiful meow while the mom got out her phone and started looking up the nearest animal rescue. "It's okay, little one. We'll make sure you're safe," she said, scratching my ears while the girl held on for dear life. This was not going as planned. Up until now, my biggest concern was getting stuck transformed as a cat. Now I was worried about being stuck as a cat and given up for adoption.

"Is that my cat?" A woman's voice came from behind us.

The young girl turned with me in her arms.

Relief washed through me when I recognized Clemmie. "It is. I've been looking all over for her. Come here, Angelica, you little rascal."

The girl set me down, and I happily trotted over to Clemmie, where she scooped me up into her arms. And darn it, I couldn't help it. I started to purr.

"Thank you so much for making sure she was okay. Stop by the tea shop, and I'll be sure to set you up with some fresh cookies."

The mother and daughter duo said they would and then went on their way. Clemmie whispered to me, "What are you up to? Sneaking into the jeweler?"

I replied with a "Puuuret."

"Let me get the door." Clemmie set me down and did just that, walking in after me. I dashed behind a display case while Clemmie distracted the employee.

"I'm so happy to see that you're open. I wasn't sure if you would be after what happened to Lyle," Clemmie said.

"For now. It was just Lyle and me. He brought me on after my apprenticeship. I did most of the online orders," the young woman said.

"I didn't even know you had a website." Clemmie looked genuinely interested. She was either interested in a website for the tea shop or better at this spy stuff than I thought. It was probably both.

"Yeah, half of our business comes in through the site. I created the online pieces, and Lyle did the work for the locals. It worked out well."

The woman held up a sparkling pendant she was working on. "Oh, Katie, it's beautiful," Clemmie remarked. The young woman beamed. Clemmie continued to talk, and I snuck around the display counters to the office.

I quickly learned that it's a heck of a lot harder to rummage through a desk when you don't have opposable thumbs. I stood on the counter and used my paws to rifle through the papers, careful to sidestep the beautiful yellow gemstone that was being set into a ring. The piece was held in place by a metal vice, a selection of tools scattered beside it. I avoided the work-in-progress and continued my search.

Under a stack of papers, I spotted a folder from the bank. I had to fight the temptation to swat the documents onto the floor. My cat instincts were fierce. The folder was similar to the one in the backseat of the rental car. Using my paws, I flipped the folder open and saw that Lyle had filled the paperwork out. I scanned the documents and was surprised to discover that Lyle was taking out the loan for his son. Maybe he didn't give him the cash outright, but he was willing to co-sign and offer collateral.

Peter was wrong. His father had believed in him. I had to find a way to let Peter know without confessing to snooping in Lyle's office.

I closed the folder and carefully brushed some of the papers back over it. Jumping off the desk, I used my front paws to grip and tug on the bottom office drawer. It finally gave way with a creak. Instinctively I ducked down. Clemmie coughed from out front. I wasn't sure if that was a sign or if she was trying to cover up the noise. I scurried under the desk and waited. After a minute ticked by, I figured I was safe. Cautiously, I stalked out and peeked my pink nose over the edge of the drawer and peered in.

A large legal-size envelope looked back at me. The words "Please sign! -Diane" were scrawled across the front. Using my teeth, I gripped at the corner of the envelope and tugged it out of the drawer. It landed on the floor with a plop. The metal clasp was firmly fastened to the back, but my curiosity was strong. Again, I used my teeth, biting the clasp to get the two metal pieces to fold back together, freeing the flap. I tried not to think about how many peoples' fingers had touched that clasp. If I did, it would only gross me out.

With the envelope open, I pulled out the top sheet. My little cat teeth left puncture marks through the paper. I read the page. They were divorce papers, along with a personal note from Diane, demanding that Lyle get on with it and sign the document this time. She claimed that she didn't want any alimony, only for Lyle to end their marriage once and for all.

"Huh," I thought, remembering Diane out to dinner last night with Roger. Maybe I was wrong. Could she have killed Lyle because he wouldn't grant the divorce? Perhaps she also assumed that Peter was his beneficiary, and that way, he would get the funds that he so desperately needed to grow his business. It was a kill two birds with one stone type situation—something to think about.

"Well, I guess I better get going," Clemmie said loud enough for me to hear. I took that as my cue to make my way to the front door. I quickly tossed the envelope back into the drawer and used my paws to shut it. Then, I crept like a cat stalking a mouse back out front. Clemmie waited to leave until she saw me. I followed her right outside the door and down the sidewalk back to her tea shop.

"What did you find out?" Clemmie asked me after I came out of her back storage room, fully human again.

"A couple of things. One, did you know that Diane was trying to get a divorce from Lyle?" I gave myself a once-over to be extra sure I wasn't sporting a tail or pointy ears.

"Really? I thought she said she didn't care if they were divorced or not?"

I shrugged my shoulders. "Who knows, maybe she didn't want people to know her private business. She's also dating Roger."

"She is? Now that's something."

"Maybe." I left my thoughts at that, not wanting to air any suspicions until I had some evidence to back it up. "I also found out that Lyle was offering to co-sign on a business loan for Peter."

"What does that have to do with Lyle's murder?"

"Nothing, but I know it'll make Peter feel better to know that his father believed in him."

Clemmie nodded. "Now what?"

I looked down at my phone. I had a text from Vance asking if I would meet him at the cafe for lunch. He wanted to update me on Aunt Thelma's case. I told him I'd meet him there in fifteen minutes and filled Clemmie in on the plan.

"Well, let me know how I can help," she said.

"Will do. Oh, one more thing. How did you know for sure it was me?" I thought Clemmie would remember what I looked like, but she picked me out in a second.

"You have a little white heart on your head when you're a cat. I saw you when you trotted on by the shop. Sorry, it took me a few minutes to come to your rescue. I was with a customer."

"Well, I'm just thankful you did."

HEATHER HAD my Monte Cristo and seasoned fries waiting for me. Not to mention that sweet peach tea.

"Thanks," I said, taking a fry and sitting down. Vance sat across from me.

"What did you find out?" I asked.

"I was looking into Lyle's financial records the last couple of days. He was financially set, and his business was well-established."

"I sort of figured that after Thelma became his beneficiary."

"Right, and that's only added to the prosecution's motive."

"How do you figure?"

"It's no secret that the inn has been struggling. Rumor also has it you went into the bank and even asked about a loan. Amber thinks that your aunt knew she was the beneficiary and killed Lyle for the money."

"But that doesn't make any sense. Why would Aunt Thelma kill him in front of everyone?"

"I know that. But, the sheriff's department has a motive, and they have eyewitnesses. To them, it's an open and shut case."

I pushed away my plate of food. I did not have an appetite at all. "One thing I can't figure is that if Lyle had so much money, why was he stressing about business being slow?"

"That was just his personality. From what I heard, he was a man that liked financial security. As business started to decline, he was worried that it would never bounce back, and he would start to lose money."

That reminded me about the divorce papers and Diane's comment. She didn't want any alimony. Perhaps it all came down to money, which is what Craig at the tavern assumed too.

Vance continued, "But even though business was slow, Lyle was still working on custom orders. Roger commissioned a necklace for two thousand dollars, and Craig had him working on an anniversary ring for fifteen thousand."

"Come again?"

"Craig had Lyle design a fifteen thousand dollar ring. I saw a copy of the cashier's check myself."

I pushed back from the table. "Come on. We need to go."

"What? Where?"

"To the tavern." I turned my attention to Heather. "Could we get this to go?"

"Sure thing," she replied.

"Can you tell me what's going on?" Vance asked once we were outside on the sidewalk.

"The day Lyle was murdered, he got into a fight with Craig. I heard Craig threaten him, and then Misty interrupted me, and I got distracted."

"You're just telling me about this now?"

"I looked into it before, but that was before Craig had any real motive. I don't know about you, but fifteen thousand dollars sounds like a decent motive for murder."

We walked into Dragon's Mead. Craig and his wife were behind the bar. One look at my face, and Craig instantly came around to the other side, ushering Vance and me back out the door.

"You lied," I said, cutting right to the chase.

"Keep your voice down," Craig replied.

"You were fighting with Lyle over the ring, weren't you?" I said.

Craig nodded. "I gave him fifteen thousand dollars. He was supposed to design a three-carat canary diamond ring. It's my wife's dream ring," Craig said the last part to Vance as if he would be sympathetic.

"But he didn't," I said.

Craig threw his hands up in the air. "No. I was supposed to get it last week, but he kept blowing me off, saying it wasn't done yet. I told him I wanted the money back. He refused. Told me all custom work was nonrefundable."

"Why didn't you say anything?" I asked.

"Because I knew what it looked like after Lyle died. I also didn't want Bonnie to find out about the ring. She would never spend that kind of money, but I wanted to do something special for her for putting up with me all these years."

"But the sheriff found out about it anyway," I surmised, remembering Craig's conversation with Amber the other day in the parking lot.

"They did, but that's all they have on me. I may have threatened Lyle, but I didn't kill him."

"Why should we believe you?" I asked.

"Because I'm a squib." Craig threw his hands up in the air again. "I can't do magic." He looked embarrassed.

I opened my mouth and then shut it because Craig

was right. Lyle was cursed to death. That meant Craig couldn't have done it.

Then I thought of something else. "Wait, what did you say the ring looked like?" I remembered the beautiful yellow-stone ring in Lyle's office.

"A three-carat canary diamond," Craig said.

"Do you have a minute right now?" I asked Craig.

"Why?" he replied.

I nodded to the jewelry store next door. "Come with me." We walked the short distance. I held open the door for the guys. Katie, Lyle's former apprentice, greeted us.

"Hi, I am Angelica Nightingale. I was in here a few days ago. Lyle showed me a ring he was working on for Mr. Daniels. It's an anniversary ring for his wife, a three-carat canary diamond?"

"Oh my goodness." Katie slapped her hand over her heart. "I had no idea whose ring that was. There's no slip or write-up by it. I felt awful."

"I have the purchase order. It's right next door in my office. I can bring it over."

"That would be great just so I can have a copy for our records," Katie said.

"I can get you a copy of the cashier's check, too," Craig added.

"No, that's okay. Your invoice has all the information I need. Now that I know who it belongs to, if you just give me till the end of the day, say around five o'clock, you can swing back in and pick it up."

"Really?" Craig's eyes lit up with excitement. "That would be great."

Katie smiled, and I could tell that she truly loved her job.

"Well, I better head back before the missus wonders where I've run off to. She's going to be shocked when she sees that ring." Craig slipped out and left Vance and me standing there.

"What about you two? Is there anything you would like to look at?" Katie asked innocently enough.

I looked down and saw that we were standing in front of the engagement rings. A sense of déjà vu washed over me. A long time ago, Vance and I had stood in this exact spot and picked out an engagement ring. That was before he broke my heart and threw away the life that we had built together.

I couldn't reply. I didn't even try. Instead, I turned and numbly walked out of the store. I continued right down the sidewalk and across the street to Wishing Well Park.

"Hey, wait up," Vance called behind me. I didn't acknowledge him. My emotions were too raw to speak. I had no idea what would come out of my mouth, or worse if I would start crying. I stood in front of the fountain and watched the water spill over, wondering what in the heck I was doing in Silverlake and if it was too late to run back to Chicago and forget everything that had awoken inside me. I had told myself that there was no turning back, but maybe I could give it a try. I closed my eyes, took a few calming breaths, listened to the water, and tried to calm my thoughts. When I opened my eyes a couple of minutes later, I was surprised to see that Vance was still standing next to me.

"That's a first," I said.

"What?"

"You didn't leave."

"I deserve that."

I didn't say anything but continued to watch the fountain. My eyes cast downwards at the coins glittering below the surface.

"I wanted to tell you that I was sorry," Vance continued.

"You don't have to apologize. It was a long time ago."

"I know I don't have to. I want to. You were right. I was convinced I had to go out and see the world, but I didn't realize that my world was standing right in front of me."

"Don't, Vance."

"Don't what?"

"You only get to break my heart once."

"Hey, listen--"

I held up my hand to silence him. "I'm sorry. I can't do this." With that, I turned and walked away. This time, he didn't follow.

CHAPTER THIRTEEN

Instead of dealing with my problems, I decided to focus on Aunt Thelma's. If I crossed Craig off the suspect list, that left Diane. I then remembered what Misty had said about the wards. Whoever had tried to break in last night at the bookstore should have blisters on their hands. That meant I needed to see Diane. The question was, when would Diane have done it, though? After her date with Roger? I supposed it was possible.

I walked over to the bakery and stepped inside. A girl I didn't recognize was working behind the counter. "Hi, is Diane by chance in?"

"Oh, I'm sorry, she's not."

"Do you know if she'll be in later?"

"No, not today. She's taking a personal day."

"Really? Well, I hope she's okay," and not suffering from blisters on her hands.

The girl shrugged as if to say she didn't know and went back to work, making a fresh pot of coffee.

I tried to think if I knew where Diane lived, but I didn't. I was sure Clemmie would know. Maybe we could make a surprise visit and take over a care package. At the least, it would provide us with a cover.

I left the bakery and wandered about aimlessly. The other thing that was still bothering me was Aunt Thelma's wand. Where was it? And what about the man who ran into me on the trail? Was he just some random jerk? I found that hard to believe, but I couldn't rule it out. I still had so many unanswered questions.

When I stopped, I found myself standing once more in front of Sticks. I went inside. Maybe Peter could help me.

"Problem with the wand?" he asked when he spotted me. I noticed Peter looked better than he had this morning. He had changed his clothes and appeared more rested.

"No, it works great. I was hoping you could help me figure something else out. It's about your dad, and I'm not too sure of my question. I guess ... is it possible to curse a wand?" I couldn't think of how else to word it.

"Yeah, sure."

"Really?"

"Of course. You can curse anything. Some of the new wands even come with built-in defense charms."

"I didn't know that."

"It's an upgrade," Peter laughed.

"Huh. Maybe that explains it."

Peter followed my train of thought. "You think my father's wand was cursed?"

"Like you said, it's a possibility."

"There's only one way to find out. You need to find the wand."

I sighed. "I know. Easier said than done." I then remembered what I discovered in Lyle's office. "Oh, by the way, I wanted to let you know. I was at your dad's shop a little bit ago, helping Craig with his wife's anniversary ring. Anyway, I saw some paperwork your father had filled out for the bank. It turns out he was offering up his store as collateral for your business expansion."

"What? Are you sure?"

I nodded. "He has the same loan folder that I picked up from the bank a few days ago. The paperwork was already filled out."

Peter turned pale.

"Are you okay?" I looked around for someplace for him to sit. There wasn't a chair in sight.

"He was going to help me?"

"Looks like it."

"I can't believe it."

"Bittersweet, I know."

Peter stared off. I let him have a moment. It would take time for him to process the info. Hopefully, one day soon, it would help him heal.

Peter blinked, snapping out of it. "Thanks for

telling me."

"Yeah. And thanks for the wand info. Not sure if you heard, but Amber arrested my aunt. Accidentally or not, I don't think she killed your dad."

"I'm sorry. I hope she didn't either."

"If only I could find his wand. I'm convinced it's key to solving all this."

"I agree, and it's suspicious no one can find it."

"Right? I think so too. Anyway, I guess I'll get going." I turned to leave. "Oh, have you, by chance, talked to your mom today? I stopped by the bakery, but they said she took a personal day. I hope she's okay."

"Uh, no. I haven't."

"Okay, I just wanted to run something by her about the festival," I lied. "I'll catch up with her later." And with that, I did leave.

FOR THE SECOND time that day, I found myself inside Clemmie's tea shop—Sit for a Spell—which was nestled between the ice cream parlor and a candy store. I would gain ten pounds in a heartbeat if I worked there.

Clemmie specialized in making her own tea blends. She had glass jars full of different dried teas that would heal everything from a headache to a heartache. I should know—she sent me plenty of care packages when I moved to Chicago.

Besides selling various teapots, travel mugs, and

accessories, Clemmie also had a refrigerated case stocked with desserts from Diane's bakery and a selection of finger sandwiches from the cafe. Guests could reserve tables on the private patio and host their own tea parties. It was a popular choice for brides and moms to be. I had attended both types of showers plenty of times in the past.

"What do you think? Will you go over there with me?" I just finished sharing my suspicions about Diane.

"I think the eagle flies at midnight," Clemmie replied with a twinkle in her eye before looking down at her watch. "Or make that three o'clock," which was when her shop closed on Sundays. "Give me fifteen minutes to close things up here, and then we can go. In the meantime, you can put a care package together for her. I have some chocolate biscotti that I know Diane loves that will go nicely with my orange spice tea." Clemmie pointed to one of the glass jars with a metal lid on the shelf behind her. Orange Spice was written in chalk on the black label. A stack of cheesecloth bags with drawstrings was next to the jars, inviting shoppers to help themselves.

I twisted off the lid and used the metal scooper to fill the small bag. When that was done, I boxed up the biscotti and then found a mug, which read "Thinking of You" in orange scripted writing, on one of the display cases, along with a red cinnamon-scented candle. I tucked it all into a wicker basket, using a coordinating brown and white dishtowel and washcloth set as filler.

The basket looked very fall-ish. You could tell that the change of seasons was on my mind. And who could blame me with all of the fall festival preparations I had ping-ponging around in my brain. I didn't see how we'd be able to get everything done in time and wondered if the town would still be in such a hurry. Perhaps I could bring it up to the committee and see how they felt about pushing back the date to the first weekend in October.

"Isn't that a pretty sight," Clemmie said, taking in my care package. "If you decide to stay in Silverlake, I could use your help around here. I bet we could sell ten baskets a day if they all looked as pretty as that one."

"I'm not sure about that. Ready to go?"

"Sure am. Let me get my purse, and we can lock the door."

I followed Clemmie out with Diane's gift basket and hopped in my rental car. Clemmie gave me directions along the way. All she had to say was that Diane lived across from the elementary school, and I knew exactly where to go. It didn't take long to get there—nothing in Silverlake did. You could get anywhere in fifteen minutes in the magical community.

I parked on the street before Diane's house, which reminded me of mint chocolate chip ice cream. The exterior siding was painted a soft green, and the trim and shutters were a warm brown. A decorative white picket fence set off the corners of her yard and contained a white Cherokee Rose. The white blooms spilled over the fence.

Clemmie and I got out of the car. The blinds were drawn, but I noticed movement in the front living room window as if someone had peeked out and quickly backed away so as not to be seen.

"I don't think she's going to answer the door," I said to Clemmie, going off my intuition.

"We could always open the door for her." Clemmie rummaged for her wand in her purse.

"You can't do that!"

"Hey, I don't know about you, but I am tired of waiting around for things to happen. This is your aunt we're talking about. We can't let her go to jail for a murder she didn't commit."

"I know, you're right, but let's knock first."

Clemmie shrugged as if to say, suit yourself.

I knocked once. No answer. I knocked louder a second time. Still no answer.

"Diane, it's Clemmie and Angelica. Will you please open up? We brought you a present." I held the gift basket in my hands higher for Diane to see if she was watching us.

"You were right. She's not going to answer," Clemmie replied, wand out at the ready.

"Sshhh, do you hear that?

"Hear what?"

I didn't have time to answer. A moment later, Diane came rocketing down the driveway in her black

WITCHY RESERVATIONS   143

Lincoln, eyes glued to her rearview mirror. She had a pink scarf tied around her chin-length, black hair and a pair of oversize sunglasses on.

"Oh no, she doesn't." Without even thinking, Clemmie pointed her wand at the car and said, "Krotos!"

A loud popping noise filled the neighborhood as Diane's tire blew. She lost control of the car and veered into her front yard. Diane was determined. She didn't stop but managed to regain control, ready to speed off once more. But Clemmie wasn't having it. She repeated the spell three more times, popping all four of Diane's tires.

Diane yanked open the car door and came charging toward us.

"Why? Why won't you just let me leave!" Diane's voice broke. She threw her hands up in the air in frustration. That's when I noticed the blisters. A few had popped, and others were dangerously close to following. A purplish liquid oozed out of the open sores.

"Why did you do it? Was it because Lyle wouldn't give you a divorce?" I asked.

"What on earth are you talking about?" Diane asked.

"Kill Lyle. It was you that cursed his wand and tried to break into the bookstore last night to get it back." At least that's the way I thought it went down.

"I admit to trying to break into the bookstore, but I didn't kill Lyle."

"Then, why run?" Clemmie's arms were folded across her chest, her wand was still out, and she was ready to strike at a moment's notice.

"And why go back for the wand?" I added.

"Because ...," Diane closed her eyes, and the tears began to fall. "Because I'm trying to protect my son."

I turned to Clemmie. She nodded in agreement. "I think we need to talk," I said, walking toward Diane and rubbing her shoulder. Diane let Clemmie lead her into the house. Clemmie unlocked the door with her wand along the way.

Diane's house was small, but her kitchen was beautiful. White shaker cabinets with plenty of storage lined her kitchen walls. The lower cabinets were topped with silver-streaked white marble. Glass jars filled with flour, sugar, and cookies sat underneath.

An icy blue KitchenAid mixer was prominently displayed in the corner next to a cookbook propped open on a stand. The color of the mixer matched the paint on the walls. A chrome gas stove and double wall oven provided plenty of space to bake. The aroma of coffee and chocolate lingered in the air, making the kitchen feel warm and welcoming.

I led Diane over to her kitchen table, stained dark like her wood floors, and set the gift basket on the counter. Clemmie rummaged around the kitchen, opening and closing cupboards looking for the teapot, and then she put on the kettle.

I found a box of tissues and plucked a couple out to

hand to Diane. Clemmie and I gave her time to regain her composure. She wiped her eyes and dabbed her nose. Finally, as the tea kettle began to bubble and whistle, Diane was ready to talk.

"Do you want to tell us what happened?" I gently probed.

Diane exhaled a shaky breath. "I suppose I have to." She was silent for a minute longer. "I guess I don't know where to start."

"How about at the beginning," Clemmie suggested.

"You're right. Okay." Diane took a deep breath. "Well, I started to think about Lyle's death and how he was cursed by his own wand. Peter is a wand expert. If anyone knew how to pull off a curse like that, it would be him." Diane looked at us knowingly. I nodded, encouraging her to go on. "Then, when I saw how strongly Peter reacted to not getting any money from Lyle's estate, I put two and two together." Diane flexed her hand and winced. The blisters looked excruciatingly painful, but she continued. "I thought that if I found Lyle's wand, I would know for certain if it was cursed. Then, I don't know. I wanted to talk to Peter."

I hadn't thought of Peter's expertise in that way, and I should've. Not to mention, Peter fit the description of the guy who stunned me on the trail. Maybe I spooked him following his father's death.

"You know, I talked to Peter today. I asked him if it was possible to curse a wand, and he told me it was. I never considered that he could have done it."

"Makes sense, though, doesn't it? You have to call the sheriff," Clemmie said.

"I will. I just need some time. I don't want Thelma going to jail, but I don't want to send my son there either."

"You can't protect him forever," Clemmie was very matter-of-fact as she poured out three cups of tea.

"I know that, but my heart is breaking. This is my son we're talking about, and I don't have any proof, just a sinking suspicion."

"You're right." But I knew that if Diane didn't contact the sheriff, there wasn't much I could do. Amber wouldn't give the theory any weight coming from me.

"So the question is, how do we get it?" Clemmie asked.

"Proof? We come up with a plan." And I might just have one.

W e stayed with Diane until we all finished our tea, and Clemmie put in a call to Constance to stop by and treat Diane's blisters.

"No, don't. She'll know that I've been cursed. I don't want to explain what happened," Diane pleaded.

"Nonsense! She's a doctor, and you need medical attention," Clemmie insisted, placing the call without a second thought. "Then after she fixes you up, you need to call the sheriff." Clemmie gave Diane a stern look. Diane didn't comment. I had a sneaking suspicion she'd conveniently forget to call.

After we left Diane's house, I explained to Clemmie the plan that I had brewing in my head.

"We need to make Peter think I have the wand. That way, he'll come and try to steal it, and when he does, we'll spring on him."

"Set a trap," Clemmie replied.

"Exactly, and I know just the person to help."

I called Misty and found out that she was still at the bookstore. The brown bag sale was finally winding down, and she had a few minutes to chat. I dropped Clemmie off at her car so she could run home and grab a few things before tonight, and then I went to the bookstore.

"I have a favor," I said, broaching the subject with Misty. "I think Peter might have been the one to curse Lyle's wand." I recapped how I came to that conclusion.

"Okay, I can buy that. So now what?"

"I was hoping you could stop by Sticks and casually drop that I found Lyle's wand at your store, and I'm going to turn it over to the sheriff tomorrow."

"Oooh, I like it," Misty replied.

"So, you'll do it?" I asked.

"Absolutely. If you don't mind watching the store, I'll go right now."

"Sure thing, what do I have to do?"

"Just make sure no one walks out the door with anything. If anyone gets too annoyed, freeze them until I get back."

I couldn't tell if Misty was joking or not.

"Or you can offer them a piece of chocolate. I keep a box of raspberry truffles under the counter for emergencies."

"Chocolate emergencies?"

"You know it."

"Okay, got it. And make sure to tell Peter that I'll

only have the wand tonight, and I'm keeping it in the office."

Misty saluted and left the shop, pushing the door open with her back.

Customers mulled around the bookstore, and I kept my eye on the door, both to make sure no one stole anything (like they would) and for Misty to return.

"Excuse me?" The little old lady's voice came from behind me. I turned and recognized Mrs. Potts, my first-grade teacher. She was a petite woman, well into her eighties, with a bouffant of downy white hair. "Angelica Nightingale? Is that you, my child?"

"It is, Mrs. Potts."

"I heard you were in town, but not that you were working here."

"Just filling in for a few minutes," I explained.

"Oh, you and Misty have always been such good friends."

Maybe not always, but I was trying to do better on that front.

"I don't suppose you can help me," Mrs. Potts said.

"I can try," I offered.

"I'm looking for a new recipe. Something to take to the Simmering Sisters. I want to knock their socks off." Mrs. Potts leaned in. "And prove to Loretta Johnston that I've still got it." The Simmering Sisters was a cooking club, for lack of a better term. The members all prided themselves on their culinary abilities.

"I think I can help. Follow me." I led Mrs. Potts over

to the cookbook section and pointed out a few titles, like the Potions & Potlucks I had spotted a couple of days before and Magical Meals: Make Mealtime Memorable.

"Or what about Enchanting Appetizers?" I pulled the thick white book off the shelf. The title was scrawled across the front and down the spine in a metallic blue script. I flipped it open and browsed the recipes. Unlike a traditional recipe book that listed everything step-by-step, this one simply included the ingredients and a set of spells that promised enchanting results.

"This is exactly what I'm looking for. I'll take it," Mrs. Potts said when I showed her the Million Dollar Cupcake recipe. It was a French vanilla cupcake with chocolate buttercream frosting, and gold flakes sprinkled on top. The recipe guaranteed to make the consumer feel like a million bucks, if only temporarily. Who wouldn't want that?

"Excellent. Although, do you mind waiting a few minutes for Misty to ring you up? She'll be back shortly." Mrs. Potts seemed a bit disappointed at that until I added, "And I have raspberry truffles you can enjoy while you wait."

"I can't say no to that. I'll be sitting over here." Mrs. Potts pointed to one of the comfortable reading chairs.

"I'll be right over with those chocolates."

As the minutes ticked by, I started to worry about Misty. She should've been back by now. As I stood there, anxiety kicked in, and I began to chastise myself for sending her there in the first place. What type of friend was I? Not a good one. And here I was, trying to be a better person, but no, I went and sent my friend off to set up a murder suspect. Selfish, selfish, selfish! My inner monologue continued on and on.

"Will you quit beating yourself up? People are going to think you're nuts muttering to yourself like that."

I looked behind me and saw Misty. "Oh, thank heavens, you're okay. I'm sorry, I shouldn't have asked you to do that."

"Will you calm down? It was fine. Have you ever been inside his store?"

"Nice, huh?"

"Yeah. Are you sure he's guilty?"

"Pretty sure."

"Well, that's rotten because I think he's cute."

"And charming," I added, using the word that I thought best described Peter.

"And hot." Misty laughed. "I mean, he's no blond-hair, blue-eyed lawyer, but he's not bad."

"Don't go there," I warned.

"Oh, I see the way Vance looks at you," Misty teased.

"Will you cut it out? Vance looks at me the way he looks at everyone else." I wasn't about to tell Misty what happened today at the fountain. Then she'd really have a field day.

"All right. Well, let me know when you're done being blind because Vance is still harboring some major feelings for you."

"It doesn't matter, even if it was true. Our relationship is strictly professional. Once Aunt Thelma's cleared, I won't have to speak to him ever again."

"Sure, whatever you say." I moved to leave. "Hey, what time should I come over?"

"What?"

"Tonight," Misty clarified.

"I can't ask you to do that." I already had to call Clemmie and tell her the plan was off so she'd stay home. I wasn't putting anyone else in danger.

"You didn't. I am offering. If you can't date the guy ..." Misty's words trailed off.

"You might as well get him arrested?" I filled in.

"Something like that. I'll be at your place around nine."

"Are you sure?"

"Positive. As long as you still have Monopoly."

I laughed, remembering our childhood sleepovers. "I probably still do."

"Then I'll see you at nine."

Back at the inn, I walked into the office and stopped short. Poor Allen was propped in the corner, frozen like a popsicle. I kept forgetting about the man, which meant it was time to end our relationship. I knew the breakup was coming, but I was hoping to put it off until he was back in Chicago, maybe do the deed over the phone. In case it wasn't obvious, relationships made me uncomfortable to the hundredth degree. I sighed and wondered if there was a way I could ship Allen back home in his frozen state and pay a witch in the Windy City to unfreeze him and deliver a Dear John letter. It wasn't a horrible idea, and it was very tempting if that tells you how deep my issues ran. It's a darned shame I was working on being a better person, or I might've started rounding up a crate the next minute.

I sighed in defeat.

Realizing it was never going to get any easier, I pointed my wand at Allen's chest and said, "Tixi." Instantly, his statuesque pose crumbled, and he stumbled forward. I went to brace him, and he jumped back.

"You're a w-w-witch," he stammered. His eyes darted toward the door. I knew he was about to make a break for it. His ten-key calculator be cursed.

I reacted with cat-like reflexes, flicking my wand to alter his memory. I'd meant to say "Exaleiphó" to erase the morning, but it came out as "Elapheno" instead, which apparently was a spell to turn someone into an elephant. Who knew? Allen sprouted a trunk and a tail. His body doubled in size, and within seconds I had what amounted to a baby elephant standing before me. He did not look happy. Allen lifted his trunk and blew a deafening sound.

I reacted the way any sane witch would. I screamed and ran from the office.

Percy came flying to my rescue. I pointed into the office where Allen the Elephant trumpeted once more. Percy dashed in and just as quickly back out of the office, a broad grin on his face.

"You turned him into an elephant?" Percy asked.

I nodded.

"This is even better!" Percy laughed with glee.

"Help! How do I change him back?" I shouted over the grunts and snorts coming from the office.

"Beats me. I'm a ghost, not a witch. Spells aren't my thing."

"Go get help, please!"

"From who? Animal control?" Percy laughed. "How about the circus? Or maybe the zoo?"

"Never mind!" I pulled out my cell phone and dialed Vance.

He answered after a couple of rings. "Hey, what's up?"

"I need your help. How quickly can you get to the inn?"

"Are you okay?"

"I have a spell emergency. There's an elephant in the office, and I don't know how to get rid of him."

"Come again?"

"Can you please just get here?"

"Give me five minutes."

I hung up with Vance and turned my attention back to Percy. "Keep an eye on him. I'll be right back."

Allen continued to rumble and trumpet from the office. I needed to keep him occupied.

I dashed around the corner into the kitchen and rummaged in the cupboards for peanuts. Aunt Thelma usually kept a canister or two of the dry roasted snack handy, but I couldn't find any. The only thing I came up with was microwave popcorn. That would have to do.

"Your boyfriend's on the move," Percy shouted from the lobby.

"What! No, tell him to stay." I threw the bag of popcorn into the microwave, turned it on, and then raced out of the kitchen and around the corner in time to see Allen the Elephant head for the back glass doors. I panicked at the thought of an angry elephant tearing up the town.

"Allen, wait!" I ran toward him but stopped when he head-butted the door with enough force to cause both glass doors to shake. Allen backed up and charged the doors, hitting the metal frame. I was afraid he was going to crack the inn's foundation if he kept it up. I ran back into the kitchen, where the popcorn was still cooking, and snatched my wand off the counter. My heart was pounding, and I was out of breath as adrenaline coursed through my veins. Scrambling back out to the lobby, I pointed the wand at Allen and said, "Glacio!" freezing him once more.

"Holy...cats..." I fought to catch my breath.

"You should manage the inn more often. Nothing

this fun ever happens when Thelma's in charge," Percy said gleefully.

"Gee, thanks."

True to his word, Vance arrived a few minutes later. Walking into the lobby, he looked like he couldn't believe his eyes. "There really is an elephant here."

"Tell me about it." Today was turning out to be a long day.

"Is something burning?" Vance sniffed the air.

"Ah!" I frantically ran back into the kitchen, where the bag of popcorn was burning in the microwave. I thought fast, grabbing a dishtowel and using it to whisk the burning bag into the kitchen sink, where I dowsed it with water. The bag hissed and crackled as rancid smoke filled the room.

Vance walked in after me and opened the window.

"What else can go wrong today?" I quickly shut my mouth. You never want to ask that question because the universe will show you. Things could always get worse.

"What happened?" Vance asked.

"Bad break up," Percy quipped before I could reply.

Vance looked to me for confirmation.

"He's right." I shook my head in disbelief.

"And I thought ours was rough. At least you didn't transfigure me," Vance remarked.

"Believe me, it was tempting."

Vance cleared his throat and got back to the problem at hand. "So the elephant's a person, right?"

"Yep, Allen," I said.

"Okay, then all you have to do is reverse the spell and say, adikos."

"Ah, that's it. Okay." I clearly needed a witch's refresher course. My early success with transfiguration had left me overconfident, and that was dangerous where magic was concerned.

"And the memory charm is exaleiphó, right?" I asked.

"You really don't want this guy to remember you, do you?" Vance remarked.

"Aren't you going to miss the little nerd boy?" Percy asked.

"Percy!" I said.

"What? He smells like cheese and travels with a calculator," the poltergeist pointed out.

"Good point, but that's irrelevant. Allen is a mortal. I have to erase his memory." I had only planned to erase the past twelve hours, but at this point, I was tempted to erase myself from Allen's memory permanently.

"Then yeah, exaleiphó is right," Vance reiterated.

"Okay, thanks," I said.

"Come on, Percy. Take a walk with me," Vance said.

"What? Nooooo! And miss the good stuff?" But Percy trailed after Vance anyway.

"We'll just be outside if you need us," Vance offered.

"Thanks," I replied.

After Vance and Percy were out of earshot, I set out to do what needed to be done. I worked in reverse. First unfreezing Allen, and then transforming him back into his usual self. Before he could mutter another word about me being a witch, I erased his memory, going back only to the morning when Amber arrested Aunt Thelma. When all was said and done, Allen looked at me as if seeing me clearly for the first time and said, "You know, I don't think this is going to work out." He motioned between the two of us.

His words caught me by surprise as I was going to open with something similar. "You don't?"

"Listen, you're a great person. You're smart and successful. You dress nice. Your apartment is in a great location—"

I cut Allen off. His list was strikingly similar to mine, and that was the problem. "I feel the same way about you. It was nice getting to know you these last few weeks, but I think it's best if we stick to just being friends."

"I couldn't agree more."

"It's settled then. Friends?" I stuck out my hand. Allen shook it. Then we both stood awkwardly in the lobby. I still had plenty of work to do, but I didn't know what to do with Allen.

Thankfully, he must've been thinking the same thing. "If you don't mind, I'm going to call for a ride to take me to the airport. I have a flight leaving in..." Allen looked down at his watch. "It's already five o'clock?"

"The day flew by, huh?" I chuckled nervously.

Allen's fingers were tapping away on his phone at

record speed. "I didn't realize what time it was. I'm going to have to leave right now if I want to catch my flight."

"Let me find Percy and see if he can give you a lift." I mentally calculated what it would take to bribe Percy to do me this favor. Whatever it was, it would be worth it. Double.

CHAPTER FIFTEEN

Turned out, all it took was me referring to Percy as Your Majesty for the next month for him to drive Allen to the airport. I considered that a win.

After they were gone, I walked out to the patio and found Vance sitting at one of the round tables, a can of ginger ale in front of him.

"Hope you don't mind, I grabbed a can on my way out."

"Not at all. You could've gone with something stronger."

"Maybe later," Vance let the words hang in the air like an open invitation. "Did it go okay?"

"Yeah, it did. Allen felt the same as me, so we're back to being just friends."

"Nice when it works out that way."

"It is. Thanks for your help."

"Anytime." Vance stood like he was getting ready to leave.

I stopped him. "I wanted to say I'm sorry for earlier. I shouldn't have cut you off when you were trying to apologize. In case you didn't know, talking about feelings isn't something I'm comfortable with."

"You don't say," Vance's lips twitched into a smile.

"It's just that you and I? It was rough, and it changed me." I was starting to realize that it might not have been for the best.

"Listen, I don't want me being around to be hard on you. I only want to help Thelma."

"No, I know that. I'm glad you're here. I'm the one being weird about it, and I'll try to be better. You and I are ancient history. I'm sure we've both moved on."

"Fair enough."

"Now I just need to figure out what I want. Who I am." The words were almost a whisper.

"Sometimes, it's easier than it sounds, trust me."

"If you say so. Anyway, I can't worry about that. Right now, I need to focus on the inn and Aunt Thelma. Speaking of which, how's she doing? Any news?"

"Nothing good. She's set for arraignment tomorrow morning unless someone confesses before then." Vance sounded like he didn't think that would happen.

"Huh."

"What?"

"Nothing." I didn't want to say anything about tonight's plan. I knew Vance would try to talk me out of it. "Let's hope someone does then. What time's the arraignment?"

"Ten o'clock."

"Okay, I'll be there.

Vance soon left, and with the inn empty and Misty and Clemmie not set to come over for a couple of hours, I got back to work, and by work, I meant addressing the string of emails and texts Lacey had sent me the past twenty-four hours. I never read the proposal requirements she emailed or answered her follow-up questions about how she should address some of the requests. Basically, I hung my right-hand associate out to dry. I was horrible at multitasking.

With that in mind, I switched on the no vacancy sign out front to ensure no one would attempt to check in and took my laptop outside to the patio to get some work done. I read through Lacey's email chain before opening the final proposal, expecting to find section after section highlighted with comments for me to address. Instead, I found a perfect proposal ready to submit.

I scrolled through the document and read it twice just to be sure. Lacey had outdone herself. She hadn't needed my help at all and, if I was honest, she probably hadn't for some time. The only thing Lacey lacked was confidence. Hopefully, she gained more completing the project, or she would once I told her how impressed I was. I quickly shot off an email that said all that and more, followed by one to my boss, letting her know that I was putting in a request for a leave of absence with HR to attend to some family business. I recommended Lacey take over my accounts in the meantime, citing her recent proposal submission and growth over the past two years. She was ready for a promotion. Where I had thrown myself into work to escape the past, Lacey didn't. She managed to get the job done and maintain a healthy work-life balance. I could learn a thing or two.

———

CLEMMIE INSISTED that Monopoly was for sissies, which was why at nine o'clock that night, we were sitting around the coffee table in the lobby playing three-card stud with M&Ms because that was all I could afford to lose. And it was a good thing we weren't playing with cash because Clemmie was cleaning house. The woman was a professional. Maybe I shouldn't have re-invited her over. My candy stash was dangerously low.

We left the office window unlocked but shut. We didn't want to make it evident to Peter that it was a setup. The inn didn't have cameras, but I downloaded a security camera app on my cell phone and set it up in the office. The app provided a live stream to my computer and also had motion alerts. I even upgraded to the premium service to allow the application to record the video to the cloud database. That way, it wouldn't be our word against Peter's.

Each of us had our wands out, ready at a moment's notice. We thought it would be best to look busy if Peter decided to make a move before it got too late. If he peeked in the lobby, he would think that we were all occupied and not on to him.

"Read them and weep," Clemmie said, putting down her three-of-a-kind hand. She didn't even wait to see our cards before she started collecting the candy-coated chocolates.

"So, I heard Vance came to your rescue earlier today," Misty said, stirring the pot.

"Who told you that?" I asked. Unless Percy flew over to Village Square and ratted my ordeal out, I was clueless.

"Vance was at the bookstore when you called," Misty confessed. "Something about an elephant?"

I closed my eyes.

"You had an elephant here?" Clemmie popped a few of her winnings into her mouth.

"I accidentally turned Allen into an elephant while breaking up with him." I mockingly dropped my head down in shame.

"That's one way to do it!" Clemmie laughed. "But you don't look too broken up about it."

"No, I'm not, and Allen wasn't either."

"That's nothing. You know Luke?" Misty asked.

"No. I don't know any Lukes." I replied.

"Really? He owns the candy shop next to me," Clemmie said.

"I thought the Rigattis owned that," I commented.

"Not for the last five years," Clemmie said.

"Anyway, he broke up with his girlfriend, and she turned him into a toad. Like a real, warty, hopping toad," Misty said.

"I forgot about that," Clemmie remarked.

"She left him like that too! It took a week before anyone realized it was him," Misty commented.

"It took that long? Yikes," I said.

"Pretty sure she still has a warrant out for unlawful transfiguration," Misty added.

"You can get charged with that now?" I prayed Amber wouldn't find out about my mishap. She'd charge me for sure, even if Allen no longer had any memory of it.

"Not usually when it's an accident." Clemmie patted my hand, noticing the fear in my eyes.

"Sshh!" Misty held up her hand.

My computer notified us a second later that the camera had picked up motion.

"Quick!" I lunged for my wand, and the three of us snuck down the hall. Clemmie's eyes were wild with excitement. Misty looked fierce, her face twisted in concentration. I felt sick and just hoped I'd say the right spell. With our backs pressed against the wall, I whispered, "Glacio on three. One, two—"

"Wait!" hissed Clemmie. "Glacio on three or after three?"

"On three."

"Okay, okay," Clemmie said, nodding like she got it now.

"Ready? One, two," I jumped on three, landing in the middle of the doorway, and together, we yelled, "Glacio!" Electric blue light flew from the tips of our wands, dancing about in the darkened office.

"Ah!" The man in the office shouted, but he wasn't fast enough. One of our spells was a direct hit.

I reached my hand around on the wall and flipped on the light switch. There, standing frozen in the soft yellow light, was none other than Roger. A shocked expression was etched on his face, which probably mirrored our own.

"Roger?" Clemmie turned to us with wide eyes.

"What in the world? How?" I was stunned. His appearance didn't make any sense.

"How did he even know about the wand?" Clemmie asked.

"Um, he may have been at Sticks tonight when I told Peter about it," Misty confessed, looking down at the floor.

"What?!" I exclaimed.

"Sorry! You didn't say not to tell anyone else, and, c'mon, it's Roger. Like I was supposed to suspect him?" Misty explained.

"I know I didn't," Clemmie agreed.

"Yeah, me either. I probably would've done the same thing," I said.

"Mm-hmm," Clemmie said.

"But why would he kill Lyle?" Misty asked.

We were all silent. My brow furrowed in concentration as I tried to piece it together. "Roger's dating Diane, right?"

"He is?" Misty asked.

"He is. Trust me. I saw them at The Grove playing kissy-face," I said.

"Ew." Misty scrunched up her face.

"And I also know that Diane served Lyle divorce papers."

"They were married?" Misty asked.

"I know, I didn't know that either, but apparently, it's old news," I said.

"It is," Clemmie said.

"Diane was also frustrated that Lyle wouldn't sign them," I added.

"How do you know all this stuff?" Misty asked, surprised.

"Right place, right time?" Misty didn't believe me for a second. "Okay, maybe I snooped a bit, but the rest was luck."

"And Lyle wouldn't sign them because?" Misty asked.

"Because he's cheap and didn't want to pay Diane alimony, or that's the rumor, even though Diane says she didn't want any."

"So Diane gets Roger to kill Lyle?" Misty asked.

"Or Roger took it upon himself to get rid of him," Clemmie said.

"There's only one way to find out," I remarked.

Clemmie offered to phone the sheriff's department, and I thought that was a good idea. They would probably take the call more seriously if it came from someone other than me.

"That's what I'm telling you," she said into the phone. "Roger killed Lyle, and I've got him frozen down here at the Mystic Inn. You better get here quick." Clemmie turned to us and rolled her eyes, putting her hand over the receiver. "Amber does not sound happy." Clemmie then turned back to the phone. "Oh, don't worry, we're not going anywhere," and then hung up. "I sure hope you're right about this, or we're all going to be in big trouble."

I sighed and let out a deep breath. If I was wrong, maybe Vance could give us a discounted group rate or bundle his attorney fees because we were going to need him.

"We already have Lyle's killer behind bars," Amber said when she strolled into the lobby with Deputy Jones ten minutes later.

"Will you just take your wand out of your ears and listen to us for five minutes?" Clemmie couldn't hide her annoyance.

Amber folded her arms across her chest. "Fine, what do you have for me?"

I spoke up, explaining to the deputies how I got the idea to set up the trap and use the wand as bait.

"Withholding evidence is obstruction of justice. I will gladly place you under arrest," Amber said.

"She doesn't actually have the wand," Misty said, looking at Amber like she didn't have a clue.

"Right. I don't have the wand. We only wanted Roger to think that." Well, technically, Peter, but I didn't want to complicate the story any more than it already was.

"And his motive is what exactly?" Amber asked.

"Roger's dating Diane, and Lyle refused to divorce her," Clemmie said as a matter of fact.

"We caught the whole thing on video." I referenced my computer.

"This is all circumstantial. Whereas we have direct evidence that your aunt killed Lyle," Amber said.

"Only because someone cursed Lyle's wand, and Roger knew that if the authorities found the wand, they'd figure it out. Aunt Thelma is a scapegoat here."

"They do make a case," Jones said to Amber, sticking up for us. I smiled at the deputy, thankful he was there. On the other hand, Amber looked at him like she wanted to tell him to take a hike, but she knew she couldn't.

"All right. Let's unfreeze Roger and see what he has to say," Amber said, unstrapping her wand from her utility belt.

"You guys, stay back," Amber instructed. We all took two steps back as if proving a point.

"Adikos," Amber said, pointing her wand at Roger.

Roger took in his surroundings the second he thawed and quickly held his hands up in surrender. "I ... I can explain," he stammered.

"Uh-huh, tell it to the judge," Clemmie quipped.

"Breaking in to steal a murder weapon? It doesn't look good," Misty added.

"You guys set me up," Roger said, looking at Clemmie, Misty, and me.

"Sorry, Roger. I can't let my aunt take the fall for a crime you committed," I said.

It was Deputy Jones that stepped in. "I'm going to have to ask you to come with me," he said to Roger, placing him under arrest. We stepped out as Deputy Jones read off Roger's Miranda rights. Amber turned away, clearly frustrated. Arresting Roger didn't fit into her open and shut case. I could see that on her face plain as day.

The trio of us—me, Clemmie, and Misty—stood behind the check-in counter while Deputy Jones escorted Roger out.

"I can't believe it's Roger," I said for the tenth time. "I thought for sure it was going to be Peter." I was not good at this investigator thing.

"Well, I, for one, am glad it wasn't. This means I can ask Peter out," Misty chimed in.

"Wonder if it's going to make Diane any happier to

know that it was her boyfriend that killed Lyle and not her son?" Clemmie pondered.

"Either way, she's going to need good friends by her side," I said.

"Another gift basket, coming right up," Clemmie replied.

"I think I better call Vance. See if he can get Aunt Thelma released tonight," I said.

"Good thinking. Let us know what he says," Clemmie said. "I can go pick her up." I nodded and took my phone out back to make the call.

It took several rings, but eventually, Vance picked up.

"Hey, remember how you needed someone to confess before tomorrow's arraignment?"

"Yeah?"

"Well, I think I might be able to help." I filled Vance in on setting up Roger and his subsequent arrest.

"You thought setting up a murderer was a good idea?" Vance sounded incredulous.

"Hey, it worked, didn't it? You should be thanking me."

"You realize how bad it could've gone."

"It was three against one. Plus, we had the element of surprise."

Vance was quiet on the other line, likely weighing his next choice of words, not wanting to start a fight.

I thought I'd take it easy on him and wrap the conversation up. We had just accepted each other's apology, and I wanted the truce to last longer than an evening. "Anyway, I just wanted to let you know in case you could get Aunt Thelma released."

More silence. Perhaps Vance was counting to three? Finally, he said, "I'll head down there now."

"Okay, thanks. Clemmie says she can pick her up if you think it'll be tonight. Just give me a call." And then we hung up and waited.

CHAPTER SIXTEEN

"How about I brew us some tea?" Clemmie offered.

I locked up everything tight on the ground floor, and we took the elevator up to our apartment on the third floor.

Unlike in Diane's house, Clemmie knew where everything was in Aunt Thelma's kitchen. She put the kettle on, got the teapot down from the cupboard, and prepared the loose leaf tea infuser. There was no using tea bags when Clemmie was around. I didn't even suggest it.

The rush of adrenaline from the evening's events had worn off, and I was fading fast. Talk about a whirlwind weekend. And yet, there was still something bothering me about the case.

"Oh no, what are you thinking now?" Misty read my expression.

"It's just, something doesn't add up," I said.

"I don't know. You laid it out pretty well for the deputies," Clemmie remarked.

"Yeah, Roger had motive, and you caught him red-handed," Misty added.

"That's not it." I sat and thought for a minute, and then it hit me. Roger didn't fit the profile of the man who attacked me on the trail. Roger was too old and not at all athletic. He wasn't about to go running around the lake.

"How would you describe Roger? I mean, before tonight."

"I don't know. He's a nice guy. Loves flowers," Misty said.

"I mean, physically. If you described him to the police." I clarified.

"Middle-aged, five foot seven, stocky," Clemmie said.

"Athletic?" I offered up.

Misty laughed. "Roger? No, not at all. Why?"

"Because someone stunned me on Enchanted Trail the day Lyle died."

"What?" Clemmie and Misty spoke in unison.

"I was talking to a coworker on the phone, and I didn't even see him. He plowed right into me. When I called after him, he threw a curse over his shoulder. A direct hit. I can't help but think it's related."

"What did he look like?" Misty asked.

"Honestly? Sort of like Peter. I didn't see his face,

but he was probably in his late thirties or forties. Tall. Athletic. He was wearing running shorts and shoes. A hoodie over his head," I said.

"He was up to no good," Clemmie said, standing to get the kettle off the stove. She lifted the lid off the teapot and said, "Will you look at that. I found Thelma's wand."

"In the teapot?" I asked.

Clemmie reached in and pulled it out. "It's true. Sometimes you find things where you least expect it."

"Looks like things are starting to look up for Thelma. First Roger, and now her wand," Misty remarked.

"Wait guys, that's it. We gotta go." I stood up.

"What? Where?" Clemmie asked.

"To Enchanted Trail," I replied.

"Now?" Misty asked, looking over her shoulder out the window. It was long past sunset.

"Yes, right now. We might have just sent an innocent man to jail."

Clemmie and Misty looked doubtful, but I was dead serious.

"I CAN'T BELIEVE I didn't think to check before," I said as we walked along the beaten path, our flashlight rays bouncing off the ground. In my defense, I had pretty much avoided the Enchanted Trail since the incident, but it was time to investigate what the mystery man had been up to. I had a sinking suspicion, and if I was right, it would turn everything we knew about this case upside down.

It was a new moon, which meant it was unusually dark out. With the moon blotted out, the stars shone brightly over the calm lake waters. Humidity hung in the air even though the heat had relented with the setting of the sun.

We walked along the path in a single file line as it snaked along the bend of the lake before opening back up again.

"Where did the jerk spring on you?" Misty asked.

"Not far from the residential district," I said.

"Maybe he's a local then," Clemmie said.

"That's what I thought. I lost sight of him after he stunned me."

We walked on in silence. Gone was the daylight-filled symphony of bird calls, replaced by a chorus of cicadas, grasshoppers, and frogs. A nocturnal sound-track of peeps, chirps, and plunks filled the nighttime air. Above it all, a barred owl called out from the tree-tops, the sound a combination of a hoot and a growl. I shivered and began to feel paranoid like someone was watching us. I kept my thoughts to myself and pressed on. The mission was too important to let my imagination get away from me.

"I think this is close enough," I said.

"Should we try the summoning charm?" Misty asked.

"I can give it a try," Clemmie offered, wand poised, ready to cast.

I didn't object. I still didn't trust myself.

"Okay, here it goes. Éla edó," Clemmie said, pointing her wand at the lake edge.

Nothing happened.

Clemmie cleared her throat. "Éla edó," she said, flicking her wrist. Again, no response.

"Are you sure you're envisioning Lyle's wand?" Misty asked.

"Sure as shooting," Clemmie remarked.

"Maybe we're not down far enough," I said.

"Or maybe Lyle's wand isn't here," Misty thought aloud.

"Both might be right. Let's walk down a bit and try again," I said, walking further up the path. "I'm trying to think, is there anything special about Lyle's wand?" I had only seen it that one time. I knew it was darker in color, but that was about it. And like Misty said, it's crucial to have the object you're searching for clear in your mind. It can't come to you if you're not calling it.

"It's a bit of a longer wand," Clemmie said, looking off as if picturing it in her mind. "Dark walnut. It has a single emerald, right on the base of the handle."

"Fancy," Misty said.

"He designed it himself, I believe," Clemmie replied.

"Which is probably where Peter got his love of design from," I added.

"Probably," Clemmie agreed.

"Okay, how about the three of us try together?" I suggested.

"That's a good idea. I should've thought of it," Misty quipped.

We counted off together, "One, two, Éla edó!" Our voices echoed across the lake. Before the sound reached the other side, a soft glow emanated from the lake bed. It was muted, the darkness of the night aiding in its detection.

"Right there!" Misty pointed to the sandy bottom.

Seaweed and dead leaves scattered above the mucky lake bottom.

"I see it." I bent down to the lake's edge. As soon as my hand reached in for the wand, the glowing stopped, blocked out by the murky water that had stirred. I was elbow-deep, digging through the muck with my fingertips, feeling for anything that felt like a wand.

"Do you have it?" Clemmie asked.

"No. Hang on." My fingers moved through the debris. I really hoped I'd find the wand before a crayfish found my hand.

"Glad it's your arm in there and not mine," Misty remarked.

"What are you talking about. You're next," I joked. "Wait, hang on." I pulled up my hand. Clemmie shone her flashlight on it. "Nope, just a stick."

WITCHY RESERVATIONS   179

"Try the spell again," I said.

The ladies did just that. The lake bed lit up once more. I plunged my hand into the warm murky waters and came up with the wand. It was covered in sludge. Misty and Clemmie both pointed their flashlights at it. The emerald was no longer glistening, but it was there.

"It's Lyle's wand." My instinct was right. The mystery man had been hiding the murder weapon.

"Which means Roger's not the killer," Clemmie said.

"Because he wouldn't have broken in for the wand if he'd already thrown it in the lake," Misty added.

"What are we going to do?" Clemmie asked.

"We're going to have to call Amber again." A call that I wasn't looking forward to making. If I had broken any laws, she would know and arrest me for it. I was sure of it.

"You know this means they're not going to release Thelma," Clemmie said.

"You're probably right, but what are we supposed to do? Let Roger sit in jail for a crime he didn't commit?" I asked.

"I don't know. Roger still might be guilty. He was, after all, trying to steal back the murder weapon," Misty said.

"Good point. But why?" I asked.

None of us knew the answer to that, and we didn't have time to ponder it. At that moment, a twig snapped behind us, and we all screamed. I couldn't help but think that the murderer was right behind us, and if we didn't run back to civilization, we'd be his next victim.

In retrospect, it was probably a fluffy bunny rabbit or a friendly deer, but there was no way we were sticking around to investigate. We took off running like a shotgun start. In that instant, I may have made a deal with God that if He got us all off that trail alive, I'd never walk on it again.

That night I learned that not only could Clemmie play poker, but she could also outrun Misty and me. We ran the entire way back to Village Square. My lungs burned, and I had a cramp in my side. It was going to take more than Clemmie's tea to calm my nerves.

"Dragon's Mead?" I suggested, huffing out a breath.

"I'd say that's appropriate," Misty said, her breathing just as ragged as mine.

"We need us some fire whiskey," Clemmie said. "Do you still have the wand?"

I held up my hand. The dirty wand clutched in my grasp.

We walked into the tavern. The sign up front said to seat yourself, and Clemmie and Misty took up a side booth. I ducked into the bathroom to wash up and then joined them.

The bar wasn't busy. Probably a combination of the day of the week and the time of night, which was late by Silverlake standards but early by bar standards.

"What can I get you, ladies?" Bonnie asked.

"Fire whiskey. Three glasses." Clemmie held up her fingers so there'd be no miscommunication.

We all took a minute to catch our breaths. Bonnie delivered tumblers of the amber-colored liquid, and I took a sip.

Clemmie drank hers straight back. "Okay, now where were we?" she asked.

"You think there's a chance Roger is still guilty," I said to Misty.

"Don't you? Why else would he break in?" she asked.

"I don't know. He wanted that wand, though, that's for sure," I said.

"Mmm-hmm. I say we wait to call Amber. Give her a chance to talk to Roger. Maybe it was a two-man job," Clemmie said.

"You know what this means? Peter could still be the killer." I hated to say that, but it was true.

"He didn't show up tonight!" Clemmie said.

"And he wouldn't because he'd know the wand wasn't at the bookstore," I said.

"Does that mean he knows that we're on to him?" Clemmie asked.

"I hope not. If Peter asks, I'm going to say that I found a wand that I thought was Lyle's, but it turned out to belong to someone else," I said.

"Good thinking," Clemmie replied.

"Shoot," Misty said.

"What, what is it?" I asked.

"I liked it better when Roger was the bad guy," Misty replied.

"Yeah, I guess I did too." Suddenly I knew how Amber felt. The case wasn't nice and tidy anymore, if it ever was.

"Good news," Vance said when I answered the phone. "Roger confessed. He said he was trying to steal the wand to cover his tracks. They're letting your aunt go."

I didn't speak. I wasn't sure what to say.

"Angie?" Vance asked.

"Sorry, there's only one problem." I grimaced.

"What? "Vance asked.

"Roger's not the killer."

"What? How do you know?" Vance's voice was quieter, as if he didn't want anyone to overhear our conversation.

"We just found Lyle's wand in the lake. Remember that guy on Enchanted Trail? He was trying to get rid of the murder weapon. Roger would know that if he was the killer."

"Shoot," Vance said.

"Which means Roger's covering for someone," I said.

"Who? Diane?" Vance asked.

"No. I talked to her earlier, and she thought Peter was guilty. That's who the trap was initially set up for. We expected Peter would show to steal the wand, but he didn't."

"So he could still be the killer," Vance concluded.

"Right. I don't see Roger taking the fall for Peter, though. Unless he thinks it would make Diane happy, but that seems generous." It was one thing to go to jail for someone you loved. It was another to take the fall for their adult child. "Has Roger requested a lawyer?" I asked.

"No, but I'm one step ahead of you. I offered him representation. I'm hoping to have a private conversation and find out what he's really up to."

"I know whatever he tells you is privileged information, but can you tell him Diane's suspicions? That might make him recant his confession."

"I'll do that. Thelma's still going to be released, though."

"Okay, we're at Dragon's Mead right now. None of us drove."

"Planning a wild night?" Vance laughed.

"It's already been one," and it had nothing to do with drinking.

"I'll drop her off to you guys then. She could probably use a drink. Then I'll come back and chat with Roger."

"Okay, sounds good."

"And Angie?"

"Yeah?"

"Be careful. If Peter's the killer, I don't like the thought of him wandering around free."

"Yeah, me either."

I hung up with Vance and filled Misty and Clemmie in on the plan. "Vance will drop Aunt Thelma off here shortly."

"She's still being released?" Misty asked.

"With Roger's confession, they can't very well hold her."

I thought for a minute. "Was Peter even at the book-store meeting?"

"Mm-hmm. He was there. Late, but he was there. I saw him standing in the back," Clemmie said.

"Who else? Anyone who fits the description of the man on the Enchanted Trail?" I asked.

"Luke was there. I saw him," Misty said.

"The candy maker," I said, recalling Misty mentioning him earlier. I couldn't even picture him. While I had known a lot of people at the meeting, there were unfamiliar faces, too. Too many to pick out who she was talking about.

"It was pretty busy. Some people didn't stay for the whole thing. They left before Lyle died," Clemmie said.

Hmm, maybe I should drop in on Luke in the morning. Just in case Peter's not the bad guy. I kept that thought to myself.

Vance had been right—Aunt Thelma could use a drink. She was grateful to be out of custody but more than just a little bitter about how Amber had treated her.

"Guilty until proven innocent, that's her motto," she

said, referring to the deputy. "She doesn't care about justice. She just wants to make herself look good."

"Good thing they have Deputy Jones there to keep her in line," I said. Talk about someone who deserved a gift basket.

Clemmie thought the same. "I'll drop him off something tomorrow."

After Aunt Thelma's drink, we were ready to head back to the inn. This time, we skipped the Enchanted Trail and walked the short distance on the main road, power walking the entire way with our wands out.

CHAPTER SEVENTEEN

The next morning I woke up feeling like I hadn't slept a wink. Maybe I should have drunk more fire whiskey or asked Aunt Thelma to whip up a sleeping potion. I would've done it myself, but I didn't want to accidentally put myself into a coma. If I planned on carrying a wand full time, I needed to study up.

I was serious about taking a witch's refresher course and wondered if they had a mentorship program or something online. It was worth looking into or asking around. You could lead a witch to her wand, but that didn't mean she knew how to use it.

Speaking of sticking around, I still had plenty of work to do at the hotel. I spent the morning working in the office. I thought I figured out which computer system to purchase for the front desk and the reservation software we were going to go with. I also thought a business credit card would be a smart idea, especially since I was ordering everything online. The night before, Aunt Thelma had told me to go ahead and buy whatever I thought was best. She also agreed to keep her personal finances separate from the inn's, something she had never done.

Amazingly, in the short time he was at the inn, Allen had balanced the books, and everything was in the black—but barely. Of course, Aunt Thelma had recently inherited money. However, when I suggested we spend it on the hotel upgrades, she insisted on still applying for a loan, saying she wasn't comfortable spending Lyle's money on her business. I didn't argue. It was a sensitive subject, and I respected that.

Unfortunately, I didn't want to waste any time waiting to complete the upgrade. Seeing we were inviting all our former guests for the festival, we needed to put our best foot forward if the inn was going to see the occupancy rate it had ten years ago.

Whereas I hadn't slept at all, it seemed like that was all Aunt Thelma wanted to do. It was afternoon, and she still hadn't come out of her room. I had a feeling it would take a couple of days' rest to get her feeling like her regular self.

After toasting a bagel for lunch and having an iced coffee, one that I made sure to prepare freshly for myself, I asked Percy to keep an eye and ear out for Aunt Thelma and told him I was running into town.

"Would you mind doing that?" I asked the poltergeist.

"I didn't hear the magic words," Percy said in a sing-songy voice.

"Would you mind doing that for me, Your Majesty?" I amended.

"Well, since you put it that way ... no!" And then he belched.

"Oh, gross." I waved the air in front of my face.

"Thank you," Percy replied, pleased with himself.

"Percy, come on. I want to run to the bank and check something out. Aunt Thelma's been through a lot. Just keep an eye on her."

"I don't know. It'll cost you," Percy warned.

"I already called you Your Majesty," I reminded him.

Percy stood there with his transparent arms folded across his chest and tapped his toes.

"Fine, what else do you want?"

"A jelly doughnut from Diane's. Strawberry."

I opened my mouth to protest but shut it. Who cared if ghosts couldn't eat doughnuts? It wasn't my problem. "Deal. Tell her I'll be back shortly if she asks."

Leaving the inn, I decided to go to the bank first and then stop by the candy shop to check out Luke. I knew nothing about him, but at this point, it was no stone unturned. I feared that Amber would show up and arrest Aunt Thelma again as soon as Roger's story fell through. I hadn't dared to tell that to my aunt. At this point, she thought Roger was guilty, and none of us told her otherwise.

After that, I'd hit Diane's on the way back home. I wasn't sure if the bakery would even be open today, and I wondered how Diane would be holding up if she was there. I was sure she'd heard about Roger by now. I should probably stop in and talk to her anyway, find out if she shared her speculation about Peter with Amber yet, or if she still planned to. It sounded awful, but I could see her letting Roger take the fall for Peter. Roger might not be willing to now that he knows Diane isn't guilty, but that didn't mean Diane wouldn't want or expect him to. Mothers would do a lot of things to protect their children, even after they were grown.

When I walked into the bank, Molly was as bubbly as ever, but at least this time she didn't hug me.

"Need to cash another check?"

"No, but I do have this loan application to drop off."

Molly looked over her shoulder at the manager's office. The door was open. "Mr. Barker is free if you want to visit with him now?"

"Yeah, that works." I headed over to the bank manager's office and knocked on the inside of the door.

"Come in." Charles was wearing a navy business suit, sitting behind his polished desk with a pen in hand, signing some documents. I had a feeling he signed a lot of papers.

"You must be Angelica Nightingale. I heard you

were in town." He capped his pen and stood to shake my hand.

I returned the gesture. "I am. I wanted to drop this application off. My aunt and I are thinking of renovating the inn a bit and were wondering if the bank might be interested in supporting us with that."

"We can sure take a look. Were you thinking of using the building as collateral?"

"We can if need be."

"That's usually the best way to get the lowest rate. Very few people have the type of liquid assets required to take on such projects." Charles' disposition changed, and his friendliness turned to smugness.

My neutral impression of the bank manager began to shift. I glanced down and noticed the title of the papers in front of him. It was a business deal between him and Peter.

"Hi, Mr. Barker. Here's that visa application I said I'd drop off," a woman's voice said.

I looked over in the doorway and saw that it was Misty.

"Oh, hey ... sorry. I didn't know you were in here with someone. I only wanted to give this to you." Misty handed what looked like a brochure over. "I meant to give it to you after the meeting, but you left before I got a chance."

"No, that's fine. I'll take it. Can I give you a call in a bit to review it?"

"Sure, that'd be fine. I'll be at the store for the rest of

the day." Misty waved goodbye to me and walked out of the office. While Charles scanned Misty's application, I looked down at the document before him. I couldn't make out the details, but there were a lot of zeros on that page. Charles was offering Peter plenty of capital.

I then looked at the bank manager—I mean really looked at him, and couldn't believe it. His physical description was an awful lot like Peter's and, thus, the man who attacked me on the trail. It started to make sense. Of course, Charles wanted Lyle out of the picture.

"Lyle wanted to invest in his son's company, but you couldn't let that happen." I pointed down at the papers on his desk. "What did you do? Curse his wand when he came in for the loan papers?"

I had expected Charles to deny it or at least be surprised at my conclusion, but he didn't do either. Charles was arrogant through and through.

"Pretty clever, huh? It was the icing on the cake when Thelma used the wand on Lyle."

Before I could even flinch toward my wand, Charles pulled his out and hit me with the same frozen charm I'd used on Allen the day before.

It was lights out.

When I woke up, I was in a tight, confined space. It was dark, and the air stifling. I was lucky I hadn't already succumbed to asphyxiation or heat stroke. Maybe that was the plan. I was without my wand. No doubt, Charles had found it in my pocket and tossed it aside before he crammed me in the trunk of his car. I figured out pretty quickly where I was as Charles turned a corner with speed, and my head bounced up and hit the metal top. I kicked and punched the metal cage in a panic, but all that did was use up my air and make my breathing ragged. I needed to calm down and think smart if I was going to escape this alive.

I remembered reading somewhere that modern cars and trucks had escape latches. I had no idea what make and model this vehicle was nor if it had one, but I frantically began searching for it. I hadn't bothered to read the whole article, figuring that none of it applied to me. When would I ever be trapped in a trunk? That goes to show that you never know what life will throw at you. I should've kind of expected it at this point.

No matter how much I felt around in the darkness, I couldn't find the mythical latch. The car slowed and turned once more, this time onto a dirt road if the bumping and gravel crunching sound was any indication. I couldn't think where exactly Charles was taking me, but I guaranteed it wasn't any place good. There were plenty of locations outside of Silverlake in the deep South where you could drop a body, and the gators would get it before the authorities ever found it. Panic started to take over. It took every ounce of mental strength to regain control. I was more than a witch. I had wits, too. It was time that I used them.

Around my neck, I felt the weight of the tiger eye. I held the marble-sized gem between my thumb and index finger. It glowed hot. I felt the magic tingle within me, encouraging me to trust my instincts. I knew what I had to do.

When Charles stopped the car and released the trunk, a revolver in his hand instead of a wand, I leaped out at him with my claws out—literally. I dug my razor-sharp nails into his face. Charles howled in pain. He dropped the gun and, with both hands, attempted to pry me off. The result was deep claw marks across both cheeks. I sprung down and took off into the wilderness. Over my shoulder, Charles lunged for the gun. Seizing it, he began shooting in the direction I had darted off to. The bullets grazed my fur. I crouched low, prowling forward, my furry belly scraping the underbrush.

Charles wasn't going to let me get away that easy, though. His footsteps were right behind me.

We were in a marshy area. Butterflies and bees hummed above. Gum trees and oaks, dripping with swamp moss, filled the landscape. The ground beneath my paws was wet, meaning there was water close by. We must be further upriver from Silverlake, I thought.

The area was abundant with wildlife. I was right. Charles was planning on shooting me and letting the alligators take care of the evidence. Unfortunately, the reptiles wouldn't have any problem taking care of a cat that got too close to the swamp's edge either. Cautiously, I stalked forward, keeping my head and tail low as to avoid disturbing the surrounding brush and give my location away.

"Here, kitty, kitty," Charles called from close by. Too close.

I froze, not daring to move. The element of surprise worked before, but I wasn't sure it would work again.

BANG!

The gun discharged, and a bird flew up into the air, not more than ten feet away. Charles cursed. He fired two more times, randomly into the muddy field, like a desperate madman.

I watched Charles through the brush. He'd ditched the sports coat but still wore a dress shirt and tie. His hair was plastered to his head with sweat, and his eyes were wide and wild. I could see his wand sticking out of his pants pocket.

If I could wait him out, I'd follow the river downstream and back to Silverlake. Plan B was to jump up and grab the tip of Charles' wand with my teeth and run off with it before he shot me point-blank. He might already be out of bullets and not realize it. It depended on if the revolver held five or six shots. I wasn't going to chance it if I didn't have to.

The ball was in Charles' court. I lay in wait.

Mosquitos swarmed, buzzing my ears. I resisted the urge to swat them away, although I was dying to. It was a slow form of torture—the insects darting in and out of my ears, biting me.

Then I heard something. It sounded like honking coming from a distance. I turned toward the noise, trying to discern if it was what I thought it was. Charles saw them before I did as he took off on foot, running scared straight toward the water.

He didn't look back. I stood on my hind legs to see what it was and couldn't believe my eyes. The brigade was coming. Vance drove his pickup truck with Clemmie and Misty in the bed, leaning over the cab as the truck bounced down the dirt road. I didn't waste any time, transforming back into my usual self and running toward them. Vance stopped. Clemmie and Misty lurched forward. A dust cloud rolled up behind them.

"You okay?" Vance yelled out the window.

"Don't let him get away!" I shouted, climbing into the back.

Vance took off. We bounced down the dirt road, Charles in our sights. Dirt blew behind us. Vance couldn't get any closer as Charles went off the beaten path, deeper into the scrub brush. I didn't wait, jumping out and running on foot as soon as Vance slowed. Vance parked and jumped out after me. I looked over my shoulder and saw he was right behind me, but Vance couldn't match my pace, and I wasn't slowing down. As if we were in a relay race, Vance handed off his wand to me in a well-timed exchange. I grabbed it from behind my back and turned up my speed.

Charles stopped abruptly. Gun in hand. His eyes darted side to side. He was stuck between a swamp and me. He looked over his shoulder and then to each side. Before he could decide, I raised Vance's wand and shouted, "Glacio!"

Game over. Charles was an instant popsicle.

CHAPTER EIGHTEEN

I thanked my lucky stars that Deputy Jones had been the one to respond to Vance's call. Amber wasn't anywhere on site. Deputy Jones was new to the department and young, but he cared about getting things right. He patiently listened while we sweated buckets under the sun, telling the whole story. I explained everything, going back to when Charles jumped out at me at the lake to how we thought it was Peter that would break in for the wand and were all surprised when it turned out to be Roger. With Roger's permission, Vance later told us that Roger thought Diane was the killer and broke in to steal the wand to protect her. His heart was in the right place, even if his morals weren't.

Once unfrozen and facing the eye of the law, Charles confessed to cursing Lyle's wand and throwing it into the lake. He hadn't known it would kill anyone, but he was reckless. At best, he'd hoped the wand would wreak havoc for Lyle and entangle him in enough legal troubles to prevent him from investing in his son's business. If he was lucky, Lyle would end up behind bars like Aunt Thelma. It turned out Charles had put an opposite charm on Lyle's wand. Whatever spell was cast with it, the opposite happened. In Aunt Thelma's case, she had intended to fully restore Lyle's health, which is why he wound up dead.

Peter and Diane had nothing to do with it. Charles knew how much of an opportunity Sticks was. He had the same vision that Peter did for the company and wasn't about to get cut out of it. Charles' crime was greed, and now a man was dead.

"But the one thing I don't understand is how did you know where I was?" It turned out to be a wildlife refuge preserve outside of town.

"It was a group effort," Vance said.

"I started to piece it together after walking out of Charles' office. I waited for you to come out, and when you didn't, I knew something was wrong. When I finally went to check, Molly said that you must've snuck out with Charles when she was on her break."

"Oh, he snuck out with you all right. Right out the back door and into the trunk of his car," Clemmie said.

"Molly was able to rewind the bank's video camera, and it recorded everything," Misty said.

"Only problem was, we didn't know where he took you," Clemmie said.

"I called the sheriff's department, but then I didn't know what to do. So I called Clemmie and Vance, and everyone else we could think of and told them what happened," Misty said.

"There's a lot of people looking for you," Clemmie added, fanning herself. Not that it did any good. We could all use a good freezing at that point.

"Then Vance suggested a tracing spell, and it worked," Misty continued.

"Sure did!" Clemmie finished.

"But for a tracing spell to work, you have to love the person," I said more to myself than anyone else.

Vance held up his palms. "Guilty as charged."

I blinked, lost for words. Misty smiled knowingly. Even Clemmie looked pleased as punch. She tugged Misty's arm, and the two walked away, leaving Vance and me standing alone.

Vance still loved me? After all this time? Well, color me surprised. I didn't know what to say or how I felt, so I ignored his confession and added one of my own.

"I figured out something, too," I said.

"What's that?" Vance replied.

"I know who I am."

"Oh yeah?" he said.

"Mm-hm." I rocked on my heels. "I'm a witch. Just don't tell anyone, okay?" I smiled.

"Don't worry. My lips are sealed."

"Good. Shall we go home?"

"Lead the way."

It wasn't until two weeks later that the four of us—Peter, Aunt Thelma, Diane, and I—were cleaning out Lyle's house that we found something extraordinary. Peter and I were emptying the dining room cabinet, wrapping up the fine china and crystal baubles, when a wooden music box on the back of the shelf caught my eye.

"That's mine from when I was a kid. My grandma gave it to me," Peter said.

"Your dad's mom?"

Peter nodded, turning the intricately carved box over in his hand. He wound up the silver crank on the bottom, and a sweet melody filled the air.

"This song always used to make me smile. I forgot about it." Peter went to open the box, but it wouldn't budge.

I was already one step ahead of him, fishing the antique key out of my pocket. "I thought this might come in handy today." I wasn't sure if it was witchy intuition or not, but I was glad I'd brought it along.

Peter slid the key into the lock and twisted. I heard a soft click, and the lid was free. Together we peered in.

"Whoa," Peter said.

WITCHY RESERVATIONS   201

"Um, yeah. Holy beautiful." I stared at the quarter-size gem. "Is that a diamond?"

"I think so." Peter held the gem up to the light and then huffed his breath on it, seeming satisfied. "I can't believe it."

"And you said your dad didn't leave you anything." I bumped Peter with my hip.

Peter was still in shock. "Guess I really did have to look within," he quipped.

"Yeah, and I'm going to comb this cabinet when we're done," I joked.

"Who knows if there are any more surprises," Peter agreed.

"I'm sure there will be." In fact, I guaranteed it.

———

READY TO READ what happens next?

Checkout Eerie Check In:

https://books2read.com/u/4DRAKg

Stephanie Damore Complete Works

Mystic Inn Mysteries
Witchy Reservations
Eerie Check In
Spooked Solid
Untimely Departure
Midnight at Mystic Inn

SPIRITED SWEETS MYSTERIES
Bittersweet Betrayal
Decadent Demise
Red Velvet Revenge
Sugared Suspect

WITCH IN TIME
Better Witch Next Time

Play for Time

BEAUTY SECRETS SERIES
Makeup & Murder
Kiss & Makeup
Eyeliner & Alibis
Pedicures & Prejudice
Beauty & Bloodshed
Charm & Deception

A DROP DEAD Famous Cozy Mystery
Mourning After

My name's Claire London and I see dead people.

Just don't tell anyone else or they'll think I'm crazy.

Er...I mean crazier.

My life was beautifully simple.

And then my husband died.

Bit of a shock when his ghost popped up.

Now there are other ghosts who need my help. I'll do whatever it takes to get them up to the Pearly Gates... and out of my bakery.

If you love a clean paranormal mystery, heavy on the whodunit, you're going to love these quick reads!

Bittersweet Betrayal

ABOUT THE AUTHOR

Stephanie Damore is a USA Today bestselling mystery author with a soft spot for magic and romance, too. She loves being on the beach, has a strong affinity for the color pink (especially in diamonds and champagne), and, not to brag, but chocolate and her are in a pretty serious relationship.

Her books are fun and fearless, and feature smart and sassy sleuths. If you love books with a dash of romance and twist of whodunit, you're going to love her work!

For information on new releases and fun giveaways, visit her Facebook group at https://www. facebook.com/stephdamoreauthor/

 facebook.com/stephdamoreauthor
twitter.com/stephdamore
 instagram.com/steph_damore_author
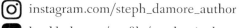 bookbub.com/profile/stephanie-damore

Printed in Great Britain
by Amazon